REVIEWS

THE ADVENTURES OF NICK AND BILLY: The Mystery of the Rougarou

"…a charming novel appealing to the young and old alike…"
— *Louisiana Bock News*

"I really enjoyed reading this story of 2, 12 year old acventures. I have a grandson who is twelve, and cannot wait to share this treasure with him! I received this book free through Goodreads, but I plan to buy copies for other middle-grade readers.
— *Nancy, Goodreads Giveaway Winner*

"I enjoyed the adventures of Nick and Billy, as they journeyed through the swamp. I hated the few times I had to put this book down. It is a book I will read again and that says a lot about the quality of the writing. I found the characters the good and evil ones to be an integral part of the story. The Mystery of the Rougarou: A Nick Landry and.. by Michael Hoard is suspenseful, adventurous and a well written story.
This book is what reading is all about. Getting lost in the swamp and the characters. Definitely, hoping this becomes a series!"
— *Tar Heel*

"I have to say you depicted the area and the people down here in the swamp better than anyone else has. Your book was wonderful and it stirred feelings up that everyone down here has had at one or more times in their life. Its sad to say that this a fairly common problem we have with getting lost in the swamps. I would give it a six if there was more. Please tell me that we will hear more from the Landry and Boudreaux boys."
— *Brent Wengert*

A FORSAKEN SOUL

"Brilliant and brutal! This story is written by a very special writer with the ability to transport the reader inside the lead character and I couldn't put it down…the best story I have read for many years. Everyone should read this…
— *Richard, Cambridgeshire, UK, Goodreads Giveaway Winnner*

THE ADVENTURES OF NICK AND BILLY

AND BILLY

-The Mystery of the Rougarou

By MICHAEL HOARD

Edited by Gayla LaBry

Cover art created by RM Designs

Published by
Biblio Publishing
Columbus, Ohio

ISBN: 978-1-62249-382-1

Written and printed in the United States of America

Dedicated to
Kathy Marie Hoard
An adventurous soul that will always
be connected to my own.

ACKNOWLEDGMENTS

There are countless people – both friends and strangers – that are responsible for encouraging me to continue writing. You are my friends, work colleagues, and visitors online who, by showing your enthusiasm in my writing, unknowingly feed my desire to create stories to entertain and remember. Your comments and belief in me will always be appreciated.

As always, first and foremost, is my wife, friend, and soulmate, Kathy. She is my dream-come-true, keeping the adventure in my life and love in my heart.

Katie and Lou Caggiano, my daughter and son-in-law, who share their love and affections so freely.

Danielle and Wolfgang Lawton, my daughter and son-in-law, who have recently blessed me with two beautiful granddaughters.

Mom, dad, brother and sister who have always provided me with everything necessary to grow into the man I am today…and never abandoning me during my rambunctious teen years.

Barbara Hoard and Wesley Webster, two people whose kindness and good hearts will always be cherished by me.

The numerous family I have scattered in Tennessee, Texas, Indiana, Florida, Georgia, and New York who are the best a man could ask for in a family.

Ethan (E-Man) Thomas, my 10-year-old Quality Assurance Expert that assured me that this book is awesome.

Gayla LaBry, my editor and friend, whose magic with words and sentence structure makes it possible for you to enjoy my stories. If it weren't for her I'm sure I'd be beat up pretty bad on my website.

Cheré Coen, author, journalist, reviewer for Louisiana Book News, for her insight in what it takes to be published today. Your advice and experience are much appreciated.

Contents

A Map drawn by Sheriff Leger to show the route the boys took on their Adventure

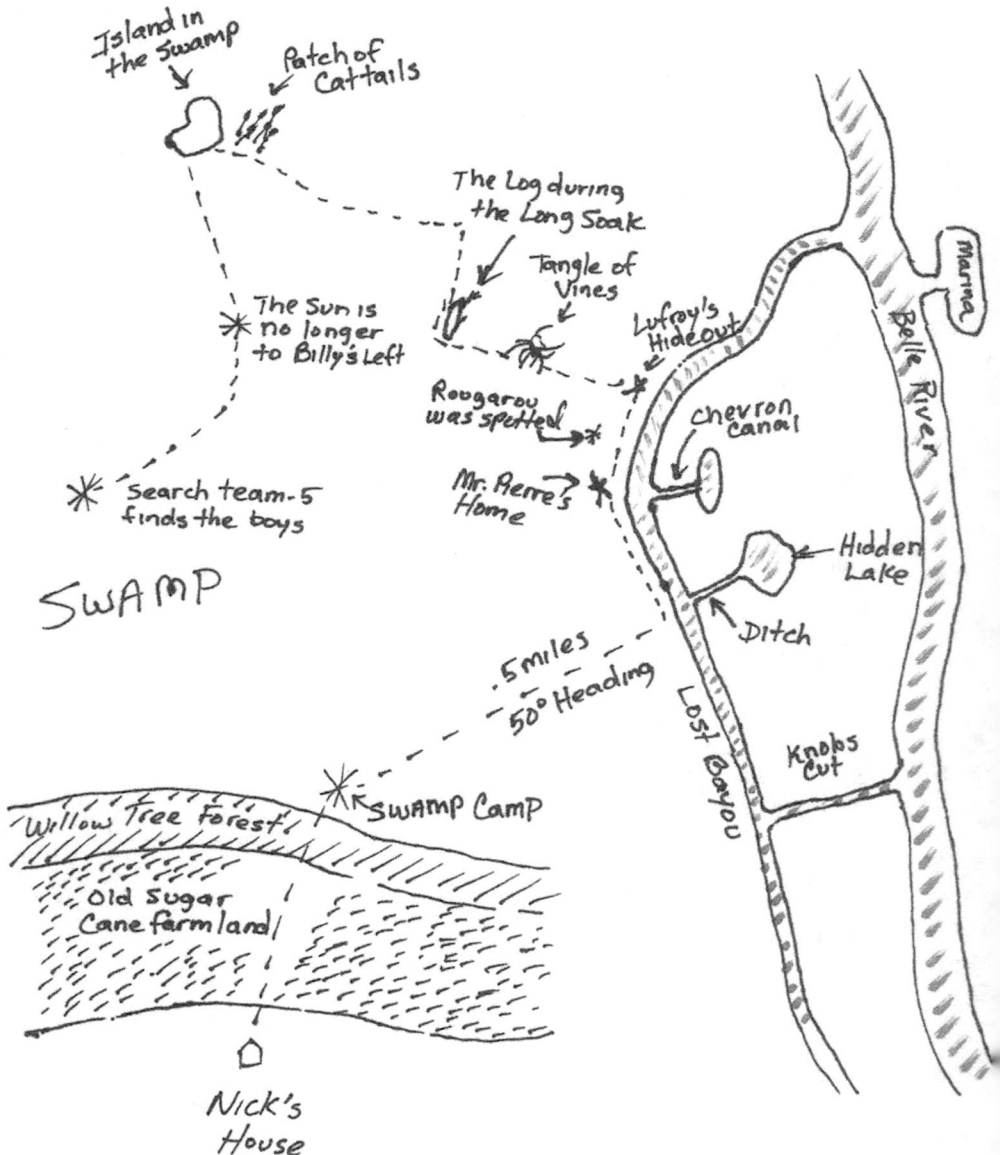

Island in the Swamp

Patch of Cattails

The Log during the Long Soak

Tangle of Vines

Lufroy's Hideout

The Sun is no longer to Billy's Left

Rougarou was spotted

Chevron canal

Mr. Pierre's Home

Hidden Lake

Search team-5 finds the boys

Ditch

SWAMP

Marina

Belle River

.5 miles
50° Heading

Lost Bayou

Knobs Cut

Willow Tree Forest

Swamp Camp

Old Sugar Cane farm land

Nick's House

CHAPTER 1

Swamp Camp

Billy Boudreaux and Nick Landry have been best friends since the day Nick was taken home from the hospital, two days after he was born. Billy was only three months old himself at the time and from the first moment their eyes made contact, it was silently understood by both boys that they would be best friends forever. And so it was.

As the boys got older, their character and beliefs began to take shape. Both boys have been raised in similar homes with similar beliefs. Respect, honesty, hard work, and family values, being key lessons for them both. They'd take it upon themselves to offer assistance to the elderly, whether carrying groceries, helping them walk across the street, or offering to cut their grass. They'd have friendly competition amongst their friends to see who would receive the best grade in class. They'd compete in sports, and most important, they'd often help each other complete their chores in order to get outside for playtime all the quicker. And never was this more important than now—the first day of summer vacation!

They're helping each other now. Billy's wiping down Nick's dresser while Nick's putting the last of his dirty clothes into the hamper. They've developed a teammate mentality for doing this, no matter whose room they're working on, and they don't need words to get it done. They each know their own duty and that the more talking that goes on, the longer it'll take to get outside to begin the day's adventure.

"Done," says Nick.

"Mission completed here," Billy replies.

And with that, both boys race out of the bedroom. While running down the hallway, Nick shouts, "Done, Mom, heading out back!" They all know that *heading out back* means the boys are heading out to Swamp Camp.

As the boys let the patio door slam shut behind them, they sit side by side on the outside bench to put on their rubber boots. "Be back before dark!" Nick's mom shouts. They both know this house rule so they don't skip a beat as they pull on their boots, fasten their machete holsters to their belts, and begin racing for the trail at the edge of Nick's backyard, where the manicured lawn meets waist-high field-grass. It's obvious that the grassy field is nothing more than an old, overgrown sugar cane farm. Long before the boys were born, a farmer had worked this land and those rows that the farmer last plowed are still there today, forty-five years later. The grass is thick and looking down toward the trail you can see quite a few rabbit trails exiting the wild growth, forming intersections with the human trail. In fact, early in the morning, when the dewdrops still sit beaded up on the grass, you can always spot a wild swamp rabbit, or two, enjoying an early morning meal of tender, new grass that has come out of the ground during the night. During rabbit hunting season the boys build rabbit traps out of old cypress boards and place them off to the side of these trails. Oftentimes, rabbits, looking to take overnight refuge from predators such as bobcats and mink, will enter these traps thinking they're old logs. When they walk into the trigger, the door will shut, promising the boys one of their favorite meals—fresh rabbit cooked down in dark gravy and served over rice.

About one hundred yards down the trail, Billy and Nick slow down to a walk. This is the point where tall field-grass changes to a dense forest of willow trees. Patches of blackberry bushes, ranging in size from that of a small dog to as big as a house, are scattered among the trees. The hard dirt-packed trail also begins to dampen, and pools of water can be spotted off to either side. The sounds of nature intensify here. The sounds of grasshoppers, crickets, frogs, and birds come together to create a symphony of musical bliss that puts the boys in a state of wonderment and peace.

This is their favorite spot for hunting woodcock. The small marsh bird with a long pointy beak spends his day foraging in the wet marshy ground within the willow trees for insects and worms. As the sun begins to set, these birds take flight and head off to their roosting area for the night. The boys don't know exactly where the birds sleep, but they can always count on them flying over this trail to get there. Though the hunting season doesn't last long, it's always an exciting time for the boys, not to mention their taste buds can never get enough of the thick, tasty meat these birds provide for their families' dinner table.

The boys bend down to pick up the walking sticks that they always leave at this important juncture in the trail. Their main reason for using the sticks is for balance. In another one hundred feet or so, where the dampened trail is swallowed up by swamp water, the willow forest will give way to wild pecan, oak, cedar, and cypress trees. The cypress knees that grow out of the ground like stalagmite in a cave are often not visible because of the water. Tripping on these hard root-like knees has caused these young swamp adventurers to splash face-first into the water on more than one occasion. To avoid future encounters with these hidden tree growths, they needed a warning system of sorts. Hence the walking sticks. They also use their walking sticks to clear spiders and spider webs from the trail. A common spider in the Louisiana swamp is the humongous banana spider. The span of its legs will easily cover the face of the unsuspecting. These spiders seem to know just where the center of a trail is and exactly how tall the next person to come down the trail will be, because it never fails, when one is not paying attention to what's ahead on the trail, he'll be totally at peace one minute, and the next he'll be screaming like a girl as he frantically tries to get this varmint-sized pest off his face before it swallows him whole!

That's the purpose of the lower, blunted end of the walking stick. The upper, forked end is their 'snake catcher.' The boys use it to pin down the head of various snakes that live in the swamp, like the common water snake, king snake, garden snake, green tree snake, copperhead, and water moccasin, which is also known as the cottonmouth.

As they pick up their sticks and begin the remainder of the hike to Swamp Camp, Nick falls back and allows Billy to take the lead. It's an unspoken agreement between the boys that Billy take the lead once there's water to trudge through. Billy's short stature naturally gives him a lower center of gravity, making it more difficult for him to topple face-first into the water should he find a cypress knee or log below the surface. When he's fully grown, he'll be short like his father and probably just as solid and powerful. Already, he's pretty strong for his age. There are no twelve or thirteen-year-olds in town that can beat him in arm wrestling. On the other hand, Nick's all arms and legs. He stands a good six inches taller than Billy and this height oftentimes gives his movements the appearance of being clumsy or awkward. But, he really isn't. Nick's hand-eye coordination helps him to excel in sports and the lean muscle in his arms and legs gives him a strength that's not usually noticed at first sight. A lifetime of walking through the swamps has helped both boys to develop leg muscles far beyond those of most kids their age. The suction the mud creates with every step they take is just as effective as weights. And, the constant necessity of clearing trails with a machete has given them both strong arms and solid cores.

As Nick follows Billy, he becomes lost in the sights and sounds around him. He notices the little things in his tiny corner of the world that most do not. He loves nature and the creatures that live here. When he was younger he would spend hours on his hands and knees watching the activities of ants and other insects just to see how they lived and what they did to survive. He was also a voracious reader when it came to books about the plants and animals that live in the swamp.

Billy doesn't have the luxury of daydreaming; his job is to keep his eyes scanning the trail ahead for spiders, snakes, or other unexpected dangers. After knocking down several spider webs and shooing a water snake off the trail, he interrupts Nick's deep thinking. "So, whose turn is it to clear the camp? I'm pretty sure it's your turn." He turns and flashes a grin at his friend.

Coming back to reality and knowing instantly the reason Billy seems so happy that it's his turn to enter Swamp Camp first, Nick responds with a great lack of enthusiasm. "Yeah, I think you're right. I plugged the holes pretty good the last time we were here, so there shouldn't be anything inside."

The general quiet returns as their boots start splashing through the water and the willows disappear behind them. In front of them, the bigger trees come into view. Because these trees have branches that start above their heads, they can see much farther ahead, and coming into sight is the best camp any kid could ever have—Swamp Camp!

Two years ago, the boys had started scouring the town for trash that could be used to construct this small structure. They'd found old two-by-fours to use for the frame, and boards to nail over the frame to form walls. They also found the perfect location, a spot with four wild pecan trees of equal distance apart in the form of a square, to serve as pilings for the cabin. These they'd hand-sawed to a height of five feet off the ground. Once the trees were cut, they began building. Not from blueprints, but from their imagination. They'd started with the frame and after framing the floor, they'd cut boards to fit. With the floor finished, they'd cut a branch off one of the pecan trees they'd just felled. They then cut this branch into two pieces about seven feet in length. They'd stuck one end of each piece into the mud and the other they'd propped against the frame, beneath what would eventually be the doorway. After hammering six cross boards to these branches and then the branches to the frame, they'd completed the stairs that would lead to the door. Now that they could easily get onto the floor they'd continued framing the rest of the structure. The tricky part of this was framing where the spaces for the window and door would be. After several failed attempts, they'd finally gotten it right. Quitting, or letting a problem beat them isn't in their character, so they'd kept at it until the problems were resolved. Next they faced the painstaking process of hand-sawing the millions of boards it would take to form the walls. Well, not actually millions, but when cutting with a hand saw in the heat and humidity of a Louisiana swamp, it sure seemed like that many. Once the walls were up, they'd used two hinges they'd found on some old shutters to attach the window, which would swing up and out, and be propped open with a stick. Next was the construction of a door using the scraps from boards and two-by-fours they'd been using all day. When they were done building the door, all that remained was to attach it to the frame using two hinges they'd found in the same trash pile where they'd scavenged the shutter hinges. This trash pile had actually seemed like a gold mine at the time because they also found some corrugated tin, which they took to use for the roof. Once the roof was nailed on, they had a real camp standing before them. Swamp Camp! It wasn't big, only about eight feet long by eight feet wide and about five feet tall from floor to ceiling. But it was a castle to a couple kids.

Approaching the camp and coming to a stop at the foot of the stairs leading into the cabin, Billy steps aside with the same grin on his face and motions to Nick. "It's all yours."

As he steps onto the first step, Nick tries to show a genuine grin, but knows his face reflects his nervousness. "I ain't scared like you," he says, sounding braver than he feels. Reaching the top step, he unlatches the clasp holding the door shut, and pushes the door open. Silence and darkness envelop the inside of Swamp Camp. Nick allows his eyes to adjust to the darkness, and then steps inside. He quickly scans the floor for any slithering shadows but sees no movement. "Hah, there's nothing in here, you chicken," he says with a touch of the bravado that recently took over.

"OK, very cool," Billy says from outside. "Go ahead and open the window so we can air it out."

Nick positions himself in front of the window, which is right beside the door. As he pushes the window out and props it open with the stick, he senses something out of the ordinary, something barely visible in his peripheral vision. Above the window they've hung an old gun rack to hold their pellet rifles when they camp out. The gun rack is a simple frame with three slots to lay their guns horizontal and, below the gun slots, a box the width of the rack that slides out so they can stash their ammunition. This is what caught Nick's attention. There shouldn't be anything on the gun rack, but his vision has detected a long fat…something. He shifts his gaze up and sees the body of the biggest snake he's ever seen in his life, and it's about two inches in front of his forehead.

The scream that precedes him, as he literally flies out of the door, sounds just like his little sister Melissa's scream that time when she'd discovered the very large bullfrog he'd placed under her bedcovers just before bedtime.

With a loud splash, Nick belly flops into the twelve-inch-deep water. As he rolls over in the water and turns to Billy, about to tell him that he'd nearly died, he realizes that this story will most likely be told around many different campfires in the years to come.

The sound of laughter erupts in the humid air, followed by another loud splash. Billy, laughing so hard he fell over, is now just as wet as Nick and the tears coming from his eyes are genuine. "Oh my God…Oh my God…Oh my God." The laughter erupts again and Billy just can't control it.

As Nick watches his friend laugh at him, he can't help but smile. "I guess that was pretty funny to see, huh?"

Billy is trying hard to bring his laughter under control. "F…f…funny?" he stutters. "Oh my God, that was freaking hilarious! I've never heard a guy sound *exactly* like a girl." As he wipes the tears from his eyes, the laughter bubbles up again.

Nick joins in. "Man, you should've seen the size of that snake!" he says between laughs. "I've never seen one that big."

Billy looks at his friend, shaking his head as he finally brings the laughter under control. "It couldn't have been that big. Let's go reclaim our camp."

They stand up, drenched and dripping swamp water. Billy takes the lead, following the snake-catching end of his walking stick. As he reaches the top step, he leans in and peeks at the gun rack. Nick, standing behind him, two steps down, sees his body tense. Billy turns slowly to face his friend. "That is one big freaking snake," he whispers. "He's coiled up on the rack. We'll both need to get in there. I'll have to lift him with the stick and hopefully be able to swing him out the door without any problem. You have your stick ready in case he's trouble."

Nick nods an affirmative and follows Billy through the door, both boys staying as far away from the gun rack as possible. Because the window is propped open, the beast snake is clearly visible. They see its huge head resting on a body that's been coiled up into a ball, ready to spring out. While difficult to judge its length, the boys can clearly see that its head is that of a water snake, which is not poisonous, but can be very mean and aggressive. And its body is as big around as a softball. Billy makes an attempt to slip the tip of the stick beneath the snake's body to lift it out. But because it's coiled up, all of its weight is concentrated in that one area, making it difficult for Billy to slip the stick beneath it. After several attempts, Billy exerts a little more pressure. The snake's finally had enough. It strikes at Billy's stick, clamping down with a vice-like grip. Billy's natural response is to pull back and that's when the real drama begins.

The snake isn't about to release his grip on that stick, but as Billy pulls back, the snake drops from the gun rack to the floor, releasing the stick from its jaws. And, then the snake goes crazy. Stretched out as it is on the floor, it's easy for the boys to see that this beast is at least seven feet long! These snakes can go from zero to sixty instantly, and when it's as big as this one is, and it's slithering straight at you in such tight quarters, you decide quickly whether to run or fight. These boys are a team who've come into the camp with a plan. There's no way either one of them is going to abandon the other in such a predicament.

Without a second thought, Nick swings into action, fulfilling his duty as backup support. Instead of jumping away from the snake, he lunges forward with the business end of the stick out front. He's able to pin down the snake's body, keeping it from moving forward. While it's crazily slithering around, but going nowhere, Billy expertly places the fork end of his stick behind the snake's jaws and pins its head to the floor, quickly and painlessly.

Out of breath from the adrenaline rush, Nick says, "OK big guy, just relax while Billy grabs you."

"Are you nuts?" Billy instantly replies. "That's not a little garden snake! We gotta figure out another way to get him outside."

"OKAY, you release his head and put your stick under him to push his head towards the door," Nick says.

While Nick keeps pressure on the back of the snake's midsection, Billy releases the snake's head and repositions the stick under the snake. Fighting the snake's heavy weight, he pushes the upper end toward the door. Nick releases the body and quickly joins Billy in ushering the huge reptile towards the door. This might not have worked had the snake not seen daylight and made his own way, voluntarily, towards the door. Its head disappears below the outside doorframe and the slithering snake seems to pull the rest of its body out and over. The task ends with a splash as it hits the water. The boys, peeking out through the door, see the snake quickly swimming along the surface, making a hasty retreat deeper into the swamp.

CHAPTER 2

MR. PIERRE

Once the excitement has passed from removing this huge snake from their camp, the boys settle in to the business they'd come out here to do—cleaning up the area around the camp. They're planning to begin overnight campouts in two days and there's work to be done. Before they can begin, however, they need to find out how that big snake had gained entry to the Swamp Camp. After a slow walk-around inspection of the exterior, the boys find nothing. After a second walk around, they determine that because the camp was built in the swamp, critters will find a way inside. So, they'll just have to continue as they have been and inspect the inside every time they come out to the camp.

"I see a lot of new vines and picker bushes that've grown up under the camp. I'll start with these and you can cut the ones you see in the area," Nick instructs.

With a halfhearted effort at bending over to look under the floor of the camp, Billy adds, "You better keep your eyes peeled under there. There's a good chance you'll find another surprise."

"Don't you worry," Nick replies with a laugh, "after that freaking monster, I'll be looking real good before I make any moves for the rest of the day."

The boys remove their machetes and start chopping. As always when it comes to work, they don't talk, but instead concentrate on the task at hand. Their grunts, from the effort it takes to chop through the occasional tough vine they come across, are audible, and their sweat quickly mingles with the water saturating their clothing.

About twenty minutes into their work, they hear the crashing of water as something much bigger than a raccoon approaches. They stop swinging the machetes and listen, their eyes focusing deeper into the swamp, in the direction of the sound. Gradually, a light colored shirt becomes visible through the trees. As the number of trees between the boys and the approaching individual decreases, a form begins to take shape.

"That's Mr. Pierre," Nick says.

Mr. Pierre Blanchard has a house about a half-mile farther back into the swamp. His father built it up on pilings to prevent it from flooding during the spring when the northern snows melt and the waters rise. If you walk forty feet straight out his front door, you'll be knee deep in Lost Bayou. Off to the sides and at the rear of his house, the swamp holds his property in a tight embrace; constantly making an effort to reclaim the area he calls a yard.

After his mother died giving birth to him, Little Pierre and his daddy lived out there alone. At fourteen he was forced to move in with his daddy's sister and her family when Pierre, Sr. was shipped off to war where he died in a ditch somewhere in southeast Vietnam. Within two weeks of receiving the news of his father's passing, Little Pierre had moved back into the house and has lived out there ever since, becoming somewhat of a recluse. He's created a living for himself using what God has provided and his daddy taught. During the spring and summer months, he runs five hundred crawfish traps a day that he's placed out in the basin. He also has numerous trout lines and hoop nets that he uses to catch catfish. And, during the fall and winter, he's a trapper. Raccoon, opossum, mink, bobcat, and nutria rat pelts all sell well.

The boys watch him crashing through the swamp. "Yeah, you're right. It's Mr. Pierre," Billy says. "Something's wrong. Why's he moving so fast?"

It's generally common practice to take your time and step carefully when walking through the swamp. Anyone who has experience in this knows that rushing through the swamp can get you hurt, or soaking wet at the very least. Mr. Pierre is carelessly swinging his legs to cut through the water as fast as possible.

As he draws nearer to the boys, they can see that he's drenched in sweat, covered with leaves, and breathing hard. There's a terrified look in his wide-open eyes and he's repeatedly looking over his shoulder, as if checking to see if he's being followed.

He comes to a stop in front of them. "Mr. Pierre, are you okay?" Billy asks.

Mr. Pierre bends over, placing his hands on his knees to catch his breath, never once looking away from the path he'd just taken through the swamp. After a moment, he turns his head to look at the boys. Close up, the boys notice the redness of his eyes and the tears streaming down his face. "*Rougarou!*" Mr. Pierre exclaims in a voice full of fear. "He's real. You boys need to get out of this swamp and don't ever come back!"

Nick wants to tell him to hush up, but knows there's no way Mr. Pierre would act this way if he hadn't seen something out there. He's genuinely scared.

The boys look at each other, not knowing what else to do. *Rougarou*, the wolf-headed, man-bodied creature said to roam the swamps looking for humans to devour, is just part of a made-up story parents tell their kids to keep them from misbehaving, like the one their parents told them. Or is it? One version of the story has it that the Rougarou is a person who's cursed to remain in this beastly form for one hundred and one days. At the end of this period, on a night with a full moon, he must draw blood from another human being to transfer the curse and free himself, though he'll remain sickly for the remainder of his days. *But, surely,* the boys are thinking, *it's just a legend.*

"But, Mr. Pierre," Nick blurts out, "*Rougarou* is just a legend. Everybody knows that."

Mr. Pierre looks right into Nick's eyes. "Boy, that's what I always thought too." His voice quivers with emotion. "But I was searching a new area for a good place to set some of my traps this fall, when I heard it behind a big old cypress tree. The first thing I noticed was the smell. It was like I had the rear ends of five skunks six inches from my nose, blasting away! As I watched, this…this…creature came around the tree and stared straight at me. It was at least seven feet tall, had two legs, two arms, and the head of a wolf! And its eyes were glowing red! I'm telling you boy, the full moon is in two nights and this thing is out hunting for someone to transfer the curse to. I'm never going back out there, you hear?"

Both boys think this over for a moment then Billy looks over at Nick. "We got enough work done out here today. Let's head back with Mr. Pierre." This is a lot to take in at once and the safest course of action would be to head home and give this some thought.

Mr. Pierre's breathing seems to have returned to normal. The boys holster their machetes and pick up their sticks to follow Mr. Pierre down the trail back towards civilization.

No one says a word until the willow forest is behind them. "I guess I'll walk on over to my cousin T-Jim's place," Mr. Pierre says.

"I'll be able to stay there until I figure out what I'm going to do. I've got nothing left now." He breaks away from the boys and heads out through the untrailed field-grass, towards the subdivision where T-Jim lives.

"What do you think?" Nick asks, as he and Billy stand motionless, watching the old timer's back rise and fall as he cuts through the ancient rows of sugar cane.

"I think it really is sad that Mr. Pierre will lose everything because of what he saw... or what he *thinks* he saw. It almost seems like a mystery, doesn't it? The Mystery of the Rougarou." He turns to look at Nick. "Hey! What say we try to solve this mystery like the *Hardy Boys* would?"

Nick tilts his head slightly as he ponders the idea. A smile lights up his face. "That sounds like a great way to start the summer!" he says, excitedly. "We can solve this, I know it! Let's start this off by looking for clues. We can go to my house and look in the newspaper to see if there's anything in there out of the ordinary. We gotta see if we can help Mr. Pierre somehow."

This new enthusiasm causes them to put some pep in their step as they head to Nick's house. After removing their boots, they head in through the back door. Nick's mom is in the kitchen. Seeing them, she says, "Imagine that, it's not even dark yet and you boys are back. Wonders never cease."

Billy stops at the entrance to the kitchen and admires the smell of chicken gumbo coming from the big pot on the stove. "Mrs. Sue," he asks, never taking his gaze off the pot, "do you have today's newspaper in here."

"You're in luck. I was just about to throw it out." Sue picks the paper up off the counter and hands it over to Billy.

"Thanks, Mrs. Sue," Billy says, already heading down the hallway to Nick's bedroom. Walking into the room, he sees that Nick is sprawled across his bed. "I got the paper from your mom."

Nick sits up, swinging his legs off the side of his bed. Billy sits next to him, places the paper between them, and starts reading. In the local section, there are a couple of stories about some out-board motors, ATVs, generators, and security equipment that have mysteriously disappeared from the area over the past few weeks. In state-wide news, there's been a decrease in highway fatalities in the past month, the state budget is being approved, there's an ongoing manhunt for Lufroy Aucoin, an escaped convict from Angola State

Prison, and the State Fair will soon be underway in Baton Rouge. There's nothing at all about sightings of a swamp monster.

As Nick sets the paper on his dresser, he turns to Billy. "We have to go out there, Billy. I think that's the only way we can possibly find any clues."

"Yeah, I know. I have to cut the grass in the morning, but we can go right after I'm done." Billy, like Nick, isn't too happy about going out there, but they have no choice and deep in their hearts they know it. Mr. Pierre's a neighbor and they need to do what they can to help him out. And right now, about the biggest help they can offer would be to possibly prove to him that he doesn't have to abandon his family home.

"I'll be at your house at seven tomorrow morning," Nick says. "I'll do the edging while you cut. It won't take us any time at all."

Billy gets up from the bed and stops on the way to the door, thinking. "You know something? My dad has an old map of this area and I don't know about you, but I'm not too familiar with that part of the swamp. After we cut grass, we can study the map and come up with an idea of how to go about the search for clues."

"I like that idea. We can get right where we want to with the map and a compass," Nick replies. "Okay dude, I'll see you in the morning. And then we're off on our first adventure of the summer!"

Billy heads out the door thinking that this is going to be great. As he walks down the road to his house, he remembers the look of fear in Mr. Pierre's eyes. The old man had definitely seen something scary out there and if it was Rougarou, things could become dangerous. Billy can't help but wonder if, this time, they might've bitten off more than they could chew.

CHAPTER 3

THE ADVENTURE BEGINS

The next morning, Nick shows up right on time. He walks around to Billy's backyard because he knows the shed is already opened and Billy's probably checking the oil in the lawn mower or getting everything they'll need laid out and ready to start cutting. Sure enough, there he is, bent over the engine with a paper towel in his hand.

Billy looks up as his friend approaches. "Oil level's good," he says. "Let's get this done so we can hurry up and head out."

"Let's do this," Nick replies as he grabs the weed eater to begin edging and cutting down what the mower can't get to.

They work quickly, but do the job right. Forty-five minutes later, they're back in front of the shed putting the tools back where they belong. When everything's put away, Billy says, "Let's go up to my room. I want you to see the map."

They enter the house through the back door and make their way to the stairway leading to Billy's room. "Good morning, Nick," Billy's parents say in unison as they come walking out of the living room. "That was nice of you to help Billy do the lawn," his dad adds. "You boys must have a busy day scheduled."

Not wanting to scare the grown-ups, the boys have decided to keep this adventure between them. They weren't going to lie; they just weren't going to tell the whole story. With this in mind, Nick replies, "Good morning, Mr. Ben, Mrs. Annie. Yeah, we got a lot to do out back today. It'll be a long day."

"You boys be careful out there and keep your eyes open," Mrs. Annie says.

"Yes, ma'am, we will. I'll see y'all later," Nick replies, as he races up the stairs to join Billy who's gone on ahead.

In his room, Billy is spreading the map out on his bed. The first thing Nick notices as he bends over the map is that a circle has already been drawn to mark the location of Swamp Camp. He laughs to himself knowing that Billy probably started studying the map as soon as he got home yesterday evening—in anticipation of this great adventure.

"Okay," Billy says, "It's going to be a long half-mile hike to get to Lost Bayou." As he points out on the map a section of the bayou with a slight bend in it, he continues, "I believe this is the spot where Mr. Pierre lives. Do you agree?"

Occasionally, the boys will take Billy's dad's fourteen-foot johnboat out for some fishing and exploring. They've passed by Mr. Pierre's place often, but comparing what you've seen from a boat to what you see on a map can be difficult.

Nick looks at the map closely. He notices something that leaves no doubt that the bend Billy's pointing out is the correct location. "Yeah, Billy, look at this. That's the old Chevron canal that comes out across the bayou from his place. That's definitely the spot."

"You're right! I figure we leave Swamp Camp and bee-line it for this point on the bayou," Billy says, pointing to a spot on the map about a quarter-mile south of Mr. Pierre's house. "From here we simply take a left and follow the bayou north in the direction of his place. Once we get there, we can just keep following the bayou north until we're satisfied nothing is out there…or we find a clue. How does that plan sound?"

"You definitely did your homework last night. I like that plan a lot."

"Then let's beat feet and go hunting." Billy says, thankful that he had put in the extra work the night before to familiarize himself with the lay of the land.

They leave Billy's house, head down the street, and cut through Nick's yard for the quickest access to the starting point of their adventure. As they walk into his backyard, Nick suddenly has an idea. "Hold up a sec, Billy. I just thought of something I want to bring." Nick disappears inside and a moment later reappears proudly holding up his hand to display some sort of canister. About the size of a coke can, it's got what looks like a long trigger running down the side, that you can squeeze with your whole hand. "Mom and dad brought this back from their camping trip in Montana last year. Bear repellant. I figure if it's good enough for a grizzly it might help if we do see Rougarou."

Billy grins. "I'm still doubtful that's what Mr. Pierre saw, but I'm sure happy you grabbed that just in case. Let's hit the trail."

And so they set out to solve the mystery of the Rougarou.

Along the way to Swamp Camp, they see three swamp rabbits that quickly dart from the main trail to disappear into the taller field grass. In the willow forest, they retrieve their walking sticks and Billy knocks down three banana spider webs, which were constructed during the night. *They sure can build them fast.*

As they arrive at the camp, Billy pulls the compass from his pocket. Both boys had been trained by their fathers to use a compass once they were old enough to venture into the swamp alone. Because their compasses are very simple and basic, they don't have a directional dial to twist to get the arrow to point in the direction they want to travel. They were taught to hold the compass flat on the palm of the hand and allow the magnetic arrow to line up with the north, then simply pick any one of the three hundred-sixty degrees that show themselves. With the aid of the map, Billy had figured out that they needed to head at an angle of fifty degrees on the compass from Swamp Camp to arrive at the point they'd agreed on, along Lost Bayou. He put the compass flat on his palm, spun it around until the magnetic arrow lined up with north and lined up the fifty-degree mark with the furthest tree he could see in the distance. He would walk to that tree and then repeat the process until they reach the bayou.

"Okay, Nick, are you ready?"

"Lead on, oh Fearless One," Nick replies enthusiastically.

Starting out, they head deeper into the swamp than either one of the boys has ever been. The deeper they go, the slower the progress. Few, if any, have laid eyes on these trees, which are hundreds of years old. They pass, and cross over, numerous dead and decaying logs. The portions of these logs visible above the water's surface are caked in poop from the different animals that use them as perches while eating crawfish, insects, and other animals smaller than themselves. Many of the logs are hollow, or partially hollowed out and used as shelters by the critters that call this swamp home.

They walk on in silence and as Billy leads the way, tall, lanky, brown-haired Nick, the deep thinker of the two, is thinking of how lucky he is to have been born in this magnificent area. He's mesmerized by the sights around him—the spider webs scattered about, a small water moccasin resting on a log ten feet off to the side, the pieces of undigested crawfish shell that are mixed with the majority of poop coating the same log, the scattered water lilies, with their purple flowers shining brightly in the early afternoon sun, and the many, many other sights that catch his attention.

Billy, the sandy-haired, bulldog of the two, is unable to look around and enjoy the sights. His single focus is like tunnel vision. He's keeping his expertly developed eyes on the path he's leading them down. Any snake he sees lying within striking distance of this path causes him to casually halt progress and use his stick to shoo it away or lift it and set it down off to the side, changing the threat into a delight for his friend behind him to enjoy.

Though he focuses intently on his task, Billy's mind falls into a hypnotic-like trance. Visions of a beautiful and smiling, brown-haired girl suddenly fill his sights, blocking out the real world. Her name is Hanna Fontenot. He can't wipe the image from his mind of how her eyes light up when she laughs at his jokes or watches him walk past in the hallway at school. She's the only thing he misses about school ending for the summer and can't wait for the next school year so he can see her everyday again. His friend Jamie is having a birthday party in two weeks and he can't wait for that either. Hanna will be there and he'll be able to slow dance with her for half the night!

"Billy! Look out!" Nick's loud shout instantly snaps him out of the sappy, fluffy, and billowy fog that thinking of Hanna has created. Billy's brain replaces the image of Hanna and her flowing brown hair with what's suspended just six inches in front of his right shoulder—a red-wasp nest the size of a Frisbee!

What had started as just a small home for a couple of wasps to protect a few of their larva, has grown and expanded into a furiously protective community of perhaps one hundred red-wasps. And at the present, they're not sitting peacefully on their nest with wings folded tight against their bodies. Every one of them has spotted the danger approaching their home, and every one of them is standing with wings straight out, ready to swarm the two big beasts that're almost upon them. Billy stops instantly and begins backing up slowly. When he's backed up about a foot, it happens.

He clearly sees the first one lift off from the nest. Then, as if they're all attached by some invisible string, the rest follow suit. "Hit the deck!" he shouts, but Nick doesn't need a warning.

These boys aren't rookies when it comes to these vicious defenders of the nest and they know there's but one escape. They hit the water simultaneously. As Billy splashes into the warm swamp water he rolls over onto his back, allowing his entire body to become submerged. He looks up at the water's surface, about three inches above his eyes, and is not surprised to see the wasps hitting the water tail first—Mother Nature's engineering to protect future generations of their species. Billy begins using his hands and feet to slide his back along the bottom, as far as he can, before needing to surface for air. He feels Nick's boot brush his hand and knows his friend is doing the same.

After about a minute of retreating below the water's surface, Nick slowly brings his face up out of the water. He looks over to his right and sees Billy's face emerge. "Man, that was close," Nick says.

"Ain't that the truth? Thanks for the warning, man. I was gonna walk right into that nest," Billy replies, breathlessly. "Let's get up slow and give these guys a wide berth."

They stand up slowly, not giving the wasps any sudden movements to zoom in on. As they back away, they can see that the wasps are returning to their nest. About half have already landed and the others are buzzing around it, remaining at the ready should the intruders be spotted again. A large log nearby allows the boys to sit down and empty their boots of water. Then, removing their pants, shirts, and socks, they wring out the water as best they can. Once they've put their clothing and boots back on, they detour in a wide circle around that nest, which brings them to a new starting point. Billy pulls out his compass to take a new bearing and sets off in the direction provided. He's now totally focused and determined to not let his mind slip into thoughts of the girl he loves.

As they make their way deeper into the swamp, the vegetation begins to thicken making travel difficult, so Billy removes his machete and starts chopping the branches and vines. As he moves forward, making progress, Nick follows, discarding all of the debris to the side to make a nice clean trail.

After about twenty minutes of steady trail busting the growth thins a bit allowing them to stop working so hard to make progress. Billy puts his machete away and they continue walking in the direction pointed out by the compass. Five minutes later, they walk out of the swamp and onto the bank of Lost Bayou.

"I think we need to remember this spot so we can follow this same trail back home later," a very sweaty Nick says.

A breathless and just as sweaty Billy replies, "Yes, for sure man. I really don't feel like busting another trail out of here."

While Billy takes a breather, Nick scans their surroundings and notices something that truly impresses him. "Good job," he says giving well-deserved credit to Billy for his navigation skills. "Look at the other side. That's the ditch we saw on the map that runs into the bayou where we wanted to come out. You brought us to the *exact* spot where we wanted to come out of the swamp."

"Yeah, I think you're right," Billy replies. "Now, if we hang a left and travel another quarter-mile we should come up on Mr. Pierre's place."

Because the bayou's edge was built up above water level and pretty much clear of debris, the boys are able to make much better time. They'll reach Mr. Pierre's cabin in no time at all.

CHAPTER 4

You Smell That?

The boys come around a slow bend in the bayou to spot Mr. Pierre's cabin a few hundred feet ahead. Their senses have been working overtime since they started following the bayou, both expecting at any moment to see the Rougarou jump out at them. "Everything looks normal to me," Nick says as they approach the cabin.

"Yeah, it does," Billy replies.

The house, a one room dwelling built of cypress boards on four six-foot pilings, was strategically placed to provide shade during the hottest part of the day. Behind it, there's a shed. Leaning against the shed are fifty or sixty fur stretching boards that Mr. Pierre uses during trapping season. Behind the shed are several hundred crawfish traps, neatly stacked, and numerous hoop nets for catching catfish. As they walk around to the front side of the house they see the old, rotting dock. Tied to it is Mr. Pierre's seventeen-foot aluminum boat.

Billy makes a quick visual inspection of the boat. "Looks like someone stole his motor."

"It must be the same thief we read about in the newspaper yesterday. I hope they catch him soon. Mr. Pierre never did nothing bad to nobody."

"They'll catch him soon," Billy says. "There's no way someone can steal around here for long and not get caught."

Pierre Part, Louisiana is a close-knit community of about 3,200 people who mostly work in the oil field or make a living off of their natural surroundings. Those who work in the offshore sector of the oilfield often leave home for up to six weeks at a time and know they can count on their neighbors to keep an eye on their property. For those who earn their living as fishermen, crawfishermen, or trappers, the tools and equipment of their trades are expensive and very time consuming to construct. So, it's a good thing the neighbors here can be counted on to report any thievery, or, oftentimes, confront the thieves from behind a shotgun. Unfortunately, the folks like Mr. Pierre, who live with no neighbors in sight, are usually the first to find themselves victimized by these lowlife criminals. Owing to the way the people of Pierre Part raise their kids and the values instilled at a young age, there isn't much crime out here…and, when a bad seed does come around, he'll soon figure out that he needs to find another town in which to commit his crimes.

"I don't see any clues here." Nick says. "Let's keep following the bayou to see if we can find anything."

Nick takes the lead and they continue their hike along the bayou. "So, Loverboy," he says turning to look at Billy, "when you gonna see Hanna again?"

"I guess at the party, just like you." It's not that Billy's shy or anything, but still he feels uncomfortable talking about girls.

"Come on man, talk to me!" Nick says with a snort of laughter. "I see the way you turn into a puppy dog around her. You ask her out yet?"

"We're just friends," Billy responds grudgingly.

When it becomes obvious that Billy isn't going to give up anything, Nick decides to not push the issue. He turns his attention to the route they're taking and silence settles around them as they focus on the mission at hand.

They've been walking for about ten minutes when Nick stops suddenly in his tracks. "You smell that?"

Billy halts with his sniffer in the air. "Yeah, smells like skunk. I wonder if we found him."

They become quiet, dreading the thought that Mr. Pierre's fears might be warranted. They drop down onto one knee and listen while their eyes carefully scan their surroundings.

Nick spots something out of place in the swamp. His first impression is that it's a snake in a tree, but after staring at it for several seconds, he realizes that it's a section of cable about as thick as the body of a small snake and it appears that a halfhearted attempt has been made to hide it. As his gaze follows it up the length of the tree, it seems to disappear into a large clump of moss. Barely visible within the moss, he sees a small dot of light caused by the reflection of the sun.

"Billy," he whispers, pointing up at the tree. "Look up there. That looks like some kind of cable and there's something hidden in that moss above it. Can you see it?"

A few seconds go by while Billy scans the trees in the direction Nick's pointing. "Yeah, I see it. What do you make of it?"

Before Nick can respond, they hear something large moving through the swamp and it seems to be coming closer. It's impossible to see it because it's not walking along the bayou, which is somewhat cleared of debris. Whatever it is, it's perhaps fifty feet from the bayou, traveling parallel to the water way, and heading in their direction.

"Hey, Nick," Billy whispers, "get that bear repellant ready in case we need it."

Nick nods and pulls the canister from his pocket, curling his fingers around the trigger and holding it in front of him like a strange looking pistol.

They remain motionless and listen to the sounds—they're definitely coming from something much bigger than a skunk—and the smell is getting much stronger. They hear a snorting sound and both boys look at one another, worried expressions showing clearly on their faces.

Nick grabs Billy's arm and points to a spot through the thick vegetation. Billy watches closely and sees a speck of movement. As the source of the noise draws nearer, they can see more of what's causing it. Suddenly, there are no longer any vines and brush separating them and it steps into the clearing. The boys' jaws drop.

It's the Rougarou! It's tall, with the head of a wolf, but the legs of a man. It's dressed in tattered pants and a dirty t-shirt. Long dark hair, caked in mud, grows from the beast's arms, and on the end of these arms are long-fingered hands with two-inch claws.

The boys are too scared to breathe when suddenly the creature stops just fifty feet from them. His snout rises into the air as if to sniff. The nose swings to the left, aiming straight at the boys, and this is when they see the Rougarou's bright red eyes looking right at them. Its mouth opens, revealing huge canine teeth, inches long. As the creature takes a small step toward them, a deep growl starts deep in its throat.

"Run!" Nick shouts, as he takes off, running back the way they had come.

Billy's right on his heels. "Oh my God, oh my God," he mutters, as they race along the bayou.

"Keep running! I hear him behind us!" Nick shouts from the lead.

Mr. Pierre's place comes into view up ahead just as a sudden crash sounds behind him, followed by a shout. "My leg's stuck! Nick, my leg's stuck in the log!"

Nick stops in his tracks and turns to see his friend struggling to free his leg from a rotten, hollow log lying across the path. Billy's weight, as he stepped on the log, had caused his foot to plunge straight through the rotting outer bark to the interior of the log. Rougarou is now only about thirty feet from Billy as Nick rushes back to help his friend. And, it's moving closer…

Just as the creature comes to within five feet of Billy, a high-pressure stream of bear repellant hits it right in the mouth. Instantly, it stops in its tracks and a loud shriek of pain explodes into the air.

Nick grabs hold of Billy's leg just above the knee and guides his foot out of the log. "Let's get out of here!" he shouts.

The boys hit the trail, full steam ahead, with Rougarou's shrieks of pain falling further and further behind. They don't even hesitate as they cross Mr. Pierre's yard to continue running along the bayou on the other side.

Billy spots the entrance to the trail leading back to Swamp Camp. "Here's the trail. Let me take the lead."

Nick moves aside and Billy runs ahead. They make quick progress in following the trail they'd previously cut. Coming to an area where the trail is no longer visible, Billy pulls out his compass. Instead of following the fifty-degree mark like they did on the way out to Lost Bayou, Billy has to find the one opposite the fifty-degree mark on the compass. The new mark is two hundred-thirty degrees. Like before, using the mark on the compass as a guide, he lines up the furthest tree he can see and heads straight for it.

Each time Billy has to work with the compass, Nick listens for signs that they're being followed. "I think we can slow down now," he says, after twenty minutes of moving as fast as they possibly could. "I haven't heard anything back there since those terrifying screams faded away."

Billy, breathing so hard that hyperventilation is a real possibility, nods and slows the pace. "Oh my God, Nick," he says once his breathing has slowed down enough for him to speak. "You saved my life. Thanks, man."

"Don't mention it. You would've done the same for me."

"That was the scariest thing I've ever seen! I don't think I'll ever come back out here again," says Billy excitedly. "A real freaking monster, man! We just saw a real monster—and survived!"

Nick remains quiet, deep in thought, considering all that's just happened.

With no need now to clear the trail, they make good time. They both sigh with relief as they spot the camp. And release a second sigh as they put the willow forest behind them and Nick's house comes into view up ahead.

"Come on up to my room," Nick says as they walk across his backyard. "I want to talk to you about something."

"I'm not sure if I'm gonna like what you have to say. I know it ain't got nothing to do with going back out there, right?"

"Let's wait till we get to my room and don't mention what we saw to my mom, okay? At least until after we talk about this."

In silence, they use the water hose to spray the caked-on mud off their boots then take a seat on the bench to remove them before heading inside. Fatigue is setting in after all of the physical and mental stress they've been subjected to throughout the day.

As they pass the kitchen, Nick's mom offers them each a cookie, which they both accept. "Thanks, Mrs. Sue," Billy says.

"You're welcome. Did you boys get the camp cleaned up and ready?"

Billy glances over at Nick, not certain what to say. Thinking quickly, Nick answers, "Yeah, Mom, we did a lot. Thanks for the cookie. It's good, just like always." He starts off in the direction of his room, with Billy in tow.

Billy shuts the bedroom door behind him. "Okay, let's have it. What's on your mind?"

After a moment to decide where to begin, Nick says, "There's something that doesn't add up to my liking. Do you remember the cable we saw in that tree?"

"Yes."

"Is that all you got to say? What's a cable doing on a tree out there in the middle of the swamp? And did you notice that shiny thing hidden in the moss above the cable?"

Billy's brain hasn't been thinking about anything that happened before he saw Rougarou. But, now, in Nick's room, with no danger remaining, he can relax. He can recall looking up and seeing the cable, and the speck of light shining through the moss.

"Sorry, Nick. Yes, you're right! It looked like the sun was reflecting off glass, now that I think about it."

"Yep, I've been thinking the same thing," Nick says. "And the only thing I can think that it might be is a camera. Do you think it's possible? Or can you think of something else it might be?"

"No, not really. It couldn't be part of an old power line because Mr. Pierre uses his generator when he does need lights. Most of the time his house is only lit with a lantern."

"Well," Nick says, "I think we need to find out if it's a camera, and if so, why is it there?"

"Oh man, I knew I wouldn't want to hear what you had to say. So, you want to just go straight back out there to where I almost got eaten? You got to be kidding!"

"You aren't going to like this, but I think the safest and smartest way to do this is to go camping tomorrow night like we had planned to do already. It's a full moon so we'll be able to see our way without flashlights." Nick pauses to take a deep breath. "Once we find the camera, we simply look around to find what the camera is doing way out there. It has to be guarding or hiding something. I seriously doubt that it's a film company doing a documentary about the Rougarou."

"What about the legend?" Billy asks. "It says that on a full moon night, after he's been infected for one hundred one days, he looks for a victim to draw blood from so he can transfer the curse. Tomorrow night could be the night!"

"But, think about it," Nick says. "The bear repellant worked better than expected. I'm sure he doesn't want a snout full of that stuff again."

"Actually, you do have me curious about this. Yeah, okay, let's do it. My dad has a flashlight with a red lens to read the compass if we need to. That'll be harder for the camera to pick up on—if it's even a camera."

"Good idea. And I'll bring the bear repellant."

Billy laughs. "Well, duhh! You'd better if you want me to go, ha-ha." After he stops chuckling, he continues, "I'm heading home to get my camping gear together. I'll see you tomorrow."

"This is turning into a summer break for the record books!" Nick exclaims.

"Well, I just hope it isn't our last one. That monster really wanted to eat me, man," Billy says.

"We'll be fine with the repellant, plus we'll have the cover of darkness," points out Nick.

"Yeah, I hope so! Okay, I'm outta here."

"Later, dude."

CHAPTER 5

Preparations

"Good morning, Mom." Billy walks into the kitchen where his mom is busy cooking breakfast.

"Good morning, son. How many pancakes do you want?" Thirty-year old Annie has the same sandy hair as her son. As a stay-at-home mom, she runs a tight ship when it comes to meal times and manners.

"Three sounds good." He turns to see his dad walking into the room. "Good morning, Dad."

"Good morning, boy." Dark-haired Ben Boudreaux, at thirty-two years of age, is a solid chunk of iron. That's what fifteen years as a welder building platforms to be sent offshore will do to you. He has an easygoing personality that the stability of family life tends to create in a man. He works hard to provide a good life for his family and he thanks God every day for the blessings he has. At times, especially when driving home after a long day at work, a tear will run down his cheek as he thinks of what awaits him at home. He's proud of all that he's accomplished and will do anything necessary to protect his family from harm.

"Hey, Dad, can I use that flashlight you got with the red light? I'd like to bring it camping with us tonight."

Ben looks at Billy for a split second before answering. "You and Nick still going out there? I bumped into T-Jim in the store last night. He told me you boys saw Mr. Pierre as he was coming out of the swamp after being scared by something."

Of course, Billy's mom hears this and voices her concern. "If Mr. Pierre, of all people, was scared out of there, I don't think you boys need to be out there either." She turns to look at her husband. "What scared him, Ben?"

"T-Jim told me that Mr. Pierre swears he saw Rougarou and that he'll never go back out there again after he retrieves his boat and a few personal items he can't get rid of. They're working on finding him a new place closer to town."

"Well that settles it," Annie says adamantly. "You boys aren't going back out there until we find out what he saw."

"Mom, please! I bet it was just a bear he saw. Rougarou isn't real and you know it. Mr. Pierre's just getting old. Living out there by himself all those years is starting to play tricks with his mind."

Annie looks at her husband questioningly. "What do you make of this, Ben?"

"I think Billy's right. There's no such thing as Rougarou, and Pierre must'a seen something that he mistook for a monster. It wouldn't be the first time the swamp played tricks on someone. Besides, it's the beginning of summer break. The boys can't turn into couch potatoes like so many kids today. Let the boys go camping."

Annie turns to look at her son. "Oh, okay, but *please* be careful, Billy, and bring your pellet gun."

Ben laughs. "I hope a pellet gun can stop a beast like that." He knows, though, that as long as the beast isn't magical, a pellet rifle will detour an attack. Once the rifle cylinder's been pumped full of air, it'll shoot a pellet out at very close to the same velocity as a small caliber rifle.

"I don't care," Annie says. "I'll feel better knowing he has it."

Billy, listening silently, wonders what they'd think if they knew about what had happened the day before? They'd probably form a posse and hunt the monster down. Billy's thinking maybe that's the best thing to do. But no, he'd given his word to Nick that he'd be there with him to learn more about the cable they'd seen, and that thing that they think is a camera.

"I think Sue needs to know about this," Annie says suddenly, picking up her cell phone from the counter, "before she allows Nick to go out there."

"Mom! Nick took a bite out of my toast," Melissa cries.

"Nick, leave your sister's food alone," says Sue Landry, as she sets a bowl of hot grits on the table. "You're lucky your dad isn't here. You know how he feels about misbehaving at the table."

Nick's dad, thirty-five year old, Sid Landry, has been gone for two and a half weeks, overseeing the construction of an oil pipeline somewhere out in the Gulf of Mexico. He told Sue on the phone last night that they were in the final stages of the operation, connecting the pipeline to the two structures it runs between. He figures he'll be home in four or five days.

As Nick is about to voice his opinion of his sister's snitching, the phone rings.

Sue picks up the phone. "Hello?"

"Sue, Annie here. I was just calling to see if Nick has mentioned to you anything about them seeing Mr. Pierre frightened out of the swamp a couple days back. Ben heard that Mr. Pierre's staying with T-Jim right now and says he'll never go back out there because he saw the Rougarou."

Sue turns, making eye contact with her son. "No, Annie, Nick has told me nothing about Mr. Pierre being scared out of the swamp by the Rougarou. What are you talking about?"

As he listens to his mom's "uh-hums" and "oh mys," Nick just knows that there'll be no camping out this summer.

After listening to her friend for five minutes, Sue finally replies, "Well, what are you and Ben doing? Sid won't be home for a few more days."

"I don't like the idea of the boys going out in the swamp, but Ben doesn't believe there's a Rougarou out there, and now that I've thought about it a little longer, neither do I. Ben doesn't want the boys camping trip cancelled because Mr. Pierre might have mistaken a bear for a monster."

"I think he's right, Annie, but I'll call Sid out on the barge to see what he says. I appreciate you letting me know about this."

Sue sets her phone down and looks pointedly at her son. "Why didn't you tell me, Nick?"

"I didn't think it was a big deal. There's no such thing as monsters. Mr. Pierre probably saw a bear or something. Not a monster."

"A bear? Is that supposed to make me feel better? They don't always eat honey, you know," Sue says with a stern look on her face.

"Come on, Mom," Nick replies, "there's never been a bear attack out there. And besides, I've never even seen one out there before. Just because Mr. Pierre probably saw a bear, and definitely not a monster, shouldn't be reason for us to stop going out there."

"Regardless I need to check with your dad first. He needs to know about this and give his approval before I let you go," she says firmly.

Nick sits silently as his mom calls his dad. He feels horrible for having to be dishonest, but it's necessary. Nick's a very rational human being and he knows that the sight of a possible camera and the Rougarou within one hundred feet of one another, in the middle of the swamp, is more than just coincidence.

He's still pondering everything that's happened during the past forty-eight hours when he hears his mom say to his dad over the phone, "No, Sid, Annie says that Ben doesn't want the boys' summer to be ruined over something that Mr. Pierre thought was a monster. Uh-huh…okay…yeah, I'll tell him…Okay, I love you, too. Bye.

Nick looks at his mom with eyes pleading, hoping that she'll give him the answer he wants to hear. He couldn't bear having to let his friend down in this. The adventure that awaited them is only a part of his worries. He doesn't know what he'd do if he has to stay out of the swamp for the entire summer. Having to stay home all summer would drive him nuts. The only place to find true adventure around here is in the swamp and it'd just drive him stir crazy if this is taken away from him.

"Your dad says to keep your eyes open and have fun," Sue informs him.

"Yes!" Nick shouts.

The relief and joy on her son's face causes most of her trepidations to disappear. She's still worried, but in all honesty, she doesn't want the boys to lose a whole summer of doing what they love. Childhood is a period in life full of magic and imaginative thinking. Unfortunately, it's only a very small part of a person's life and she doesn't want to take away any of it from her son.

"Just because you're being allowed to go, Nick," she instructs, "doesn't mean we aren't worried about this. Keep your eyes and ears open and run home as fast as you can if something doesn't seem right. Oh, and be sure to bring your pellet gun."

"I already got it laid out with my gear and a full box of pellets in my bag. Don't worry, Mom, we're professionals and we're prepared for any problem we might run into," Nick assures her. Of course, in the back of his mind he's hoping they'll be able to handle any situation.

Several hours later, Billy lugs his supplies over to the Landry house where Nick's supplies are already sitting out in the backyard, waiting to be hauled out to the camp. They each have a sleeping bag, machete with belt holster, pellet gun, and backpack loaded with water, snacks, knife, flashlight, and other miscellaneous tools that might come in handy. Billy's also packed his compass and the red flashlight they can use, if they need to, as they approach the area around Mr. Pierre's house. And Nick will carry the bear repellant in case they need it again.

Billy's adding his heap of supplies to the ones already on the ground when Nick comes out the back door. "You ready for the adventure of a lifetime?" Nick asks.

Billy grins nervously. "As ready as I'll ever be to take on a seven-foot monster, I recon."

They take their time putting the machete holsters on their belts and tying the sleeping bags to their backpacks. Slinging the backpacks over their shoulders, they pick up their guns, and head off to the trail.

As they leave Nick's yard and enter the trail, Nick looks back toward the house. "I was worried we wouldn't be able to go. That was a close call."

"Yeah, if it was up to our moms, I don't think we'd be on this trail right now. Mine sure didn't like the idea."

"That's one thing good about having a dad," Nick says, "he understands what *real* fun is. Moms were perfectly happy as kids playing with dolls and drinking make believe tea. I just don't understand how *that* could be fun. Man, I'm sure glad I was born a guy."

Approaching the spot where the walking sticks are normally resting in wait for them, they realize that they'll need to replace them, since they lost the others during the desperate escape they'd made the previous day.

Entering an area of larger trees and a water covered trail, they walk over to a dead pecan tree, blown over when a hurricane blasted through several years back, and remove their machetes from their holsters. They select two branches to use as the perfect walking sticks and set about chopping them from the tree. After shaving the smaller branches off the sides, they've got the perfect replacements.

A few minutes later, Billy climbs the steps up to the camp and quickly peeks into the cabin, making sure there are no new surprises waiting for them inside. With the window propped open there's enough light inside for them to see as they lay out their sleeping gear, just in case they need it later.

Sitting, now, on the steps of their camp, just inches above the swamp water, Nick says, "I think we should time our hike to where we get to Lost Bayou around dark. Then, we can take our time until we get to where we saw those cables in the tree. From there we can decide what to do next."

"I think that's a good plan," replies Billy. "If that is a camera, then there's no way it will give us away."

"We still have a few hours to kill before we gotta leave. Maybe we can clean up the area around here to kill the time."

They get to work, clearing the area of vines and brush. The time goes fast and the work is therapeutic, removing the apprehensions the boys have about the mission they'll be undertaking later.

As the sun begins to set, the work slows down. Neither mentions it, but they're both starting to feel nervous again. There's just something about dark shadows replacing the sunlight in a swamp that sets the nerves on edge.

"I guess it's time to head out," Nick says as the sun goes down below the horizon. "At least we'll be able to see for a little bit of the way. Let's put on some bug repellant now so we don't have to worry about it later."

Billy digs the lotion they use to keep the mosquitoes away out of his bag and sprays Nick down. He hands the bottle to Nick, who returns the favor and sprays the repellant over Billy's entire body. After this is done, Billy accepts the bottle of spray and puts it back into his bag. "Follow me, Kemo Sabe," Billy says as he holsters his machete, grabs his pellet gun, and heads off in the direction they hiked the day before.

The shadows are getting longer and beginning to win the battle of supremacy for the next ten hours or so, but the boys are able to make it quickly to where they'd previously cut a trail. They slow down briefly when they notice they're getting close to the wasps' nest and, luckily, have no problem spotting it. They once again give it a wide berth and continue on the trail.

It only takes them an hour to bust out of the swamp and come upon Lost Bayou. Their timing is perfect; it's now as dark as it'll get tonight. The moon is rising and with their eyesight adjusting to the dark they can see better than they'd hoped.

Now it's time to take a left and head alongside the bayou to Mr. Pierre's home.

CHAPTER 6

Cable Mystery Solved

They make their way slowly, the bayou releasing an eerie fog as the cooling night air meets the sun-warmed water. The insects and frogs that call this place home communicate with one another in a haunting and soulful language that only they understand. Billy and Nick are lulled into an extra sense of caution as the sights and sounds around them begin working on their nerves.

"Keep your eyes opened for alligators," Nick whispers to Billy up ahead. "They'll be out feeding and you don't want to get too close to one resting along the bank or floating in the water along the edge."

"You think I'm dumb?" Billy's whispered response is sharper than he meant it to be. "That's all I'm looking for now...until I smell a skunk, anyway."

Eyes wide open and mouths silent, they creep along the bayou's edge until they come out at Mr. Pierre's property. While inching across the property, Billy spots a huge gator beside the dock, waiting to ambush its next meal.

He stops mid-step and points toward the gator. "That's a twelve-footer at the very least, Nick. I don't recommend we make his meal too easy."

"No," Nick agrees. "Let's cut over toward the house and give him a lot of room. We can catch the trail from the other side of the yard."

And so they head straight for the house, then cut back to the bayou a good twenty yards on the other side of the gator. The entire time they're walking around the gator, they can see it tracking them with its eyes. This gator is big and old. It doesn't like to work for his food, preferring the easy ambush style, where someone, or something, stumbles upon it, oblivious to its presence. As they pick up the trail along the bayou, several glances back show the boys that the gator has not moved from where it's resting.

"Okay," Billy says, "I can't remember exactly how far we made it yesterday, but I'm sure I'll recognize the log that I got my foot stuck in. Let's move as slow and quiet as we can from here on out."

Nick nods in agreement. No speech necessary.

They progress much more slowly now along this portion of the trail. The mosquitoes seem immune to the spray, but the boys know that they're not suffering nearly as much as they would have been had they not applied the repellant. The worst part about walking in the swamp after dark is the incessant buzzing in your ears and tickles on your bare skin caused by these pesky little bloodsuckers. The natural response is to slap at them, but the boys need to remain as quiet as possible for fear of drawing attention to themselves. So, instead, they're constantly brushing a hand across every little spot on their skin where they feel an insect has landed.

After about ten minutes of this torture, Billy stops and points down. "This is the log, Nick."

Nick moves up beside Billy, looks down, and whispers, "It sure is. I'm guessing we're about fifty feet from where we started running. Let's be extra slow and quiet now."

The next fifty-foot portion of trail takes about ten more minutes to cover. After each step, the boys stop to listen for several seconds before continuing.

Nick sees it first. "It *is* a camera," he says, pointing up in the direction of the tree. "Look up there."

Billy looks up. "It's got a red light on! We couldn't see that in the daylight."

"Why would someone have a camera out here in the middle of nowhere? It makes no sense."

"I bet if we keep nosing around in this area we'll find something that ain't right," Billy responds in a whisper.

"Yeah, let's keep moving slow along the bayou and see if we can find something else out of place."

From this point on, the land is unfamiliar and they take extra care to be quiet. Somewhere in the distance they hear the sounds of an old swamp owl. Soon after, they hear the loud, frantic thrashing of water and a pain-filled screech from an animal as it hopelessly tries to escape the jaws of a gator a little farther up the bayou.

"From the sound of it, he's gonna be eating some nutria rat tonight," Billy observes quietly.

"Just keep your eyes open," Nick replies, "so it ain't us the next time."

"Have you wondered yet why we're out here?" Billy asks.

"Only about a hundred times, but you know we have no choice. We gotta get to the bottom of this since Mr. Pierre might lose everything."

"Yeah, I know, but the question still keeps popping in my head."

They continue on, making their way slowly along the bayou's edge for another hour or so when they hear something in the distance that captures their attention.

Billy stops. "You hear that? It's a motor running, I think."

"You're right. And it sounds like we're heading straight for it. It's either on the edge of the bayou or just off the bank, a little bit in the swamp."

As they slowly make their way toward the source of the sound, they hear a human voice raised in anger. It's still too far away to make out the words but it's obvious from the tone that whoever's talking isn't a happy camper. They can also see a light coming from that same direction.

"Do you want to keep going?" Nick whispers.

"We made it this far, may as well go another hundred feet, right? Whoever's arguing doesn't know we're here so they won't be keeping an eye out," Billy reasons.

"Well alright, just stay low," Nick advises. "And keep something between us and them so they can't see us."

Billy looks at his friend and grins. "I'm glad you said that, because I was planning to just walk right on in to their camp, ha-ha."

Nick grins back. "Sometimes I just don't know where your thinking is. Sometimes you're here, and other times you're in fairy land with Hanna."

"Oh, a funny guy," Billy whispers, as he turns away, unable to hold back the image that enters his thoughts for just a second, of a smiling girl. Quickly pushing it aside, he focuses intently on the trail and starts moving silently towards the light.

As they draw nearer, it becomes obvious that the light is coming from a bulb mounted on a tree in the swamp about twenty yards from the bayou. The closer they get, the fewer trees there are to block their view of the makeshift camp, which is nothing more than a shack crudely put together. On the bayou's edge, directly in front of the camp, they see a boat tied to a tree. As they approach the last of the trees along the edge of the camp, the boys can clearly see at least fifteen outboard boat motors scattered about, leaning on trees. Mixed in with these are three ATV 4-wheelers and, lined up in a row, three generators. One of these generators is being used to power the bulb that's lighting up the area, and, by the sound of it, a radio, too. Though the volume is turned down low, the boys can hear the music of an old Hank William's song.

Nick notices a table made of boards set on milk crates and what he sees on the table causes him to tap Billy on the shoulder. "Look, there's the Rougarou," he whispers, pointing to the table. "It's a costume."

Billy looks toward the table, and sure enough, lying on top is the wolf head that had nearly scared the life out of him the day before. Lying beside the mask is a pair of shoulder length gloves with hairy arms and claws attached to long, powerful looking fingers.

"And look next to the costume. That's a bottle of skunk oil!" Billy's referring to the extremely musky—and smelly—liquid excreted by the scent glands of a skunk. The oil is used—by people who can put up with the odor—as a deterrent for certain rodents around gardens. For others, it's a stink bomb ingredient. The boys are very familiar with what the bottle looks like since they once got into trouble for pouring the oil in a trash can in their classroom at school. Half of the classrooms in that wing of the building had to be evacuated. Turns out, it was much stronger than they'd thought it would be.

As they watch the area, they can hear the sound of voices raised in argument coming from inside the shack.

"For the sake of my sanity can you please stop crying like a baby, Gator Bait?"

"Look at the blisters on my face, Lufroy! Those boys about blinded me yesterday. That wasn't your everyday mace they sprayed in my face. That was extra powerful I'm telling ya. I swear, if I catch 'em, Big Bertha's gonna be eating more than my leftovers!"

"I can see the blisters, you idiot. And I've heard the same line repeated over and over since yesterday, so please, for the love of God, just shut your trap and suffer in silence! And you better toughen up. Remember, we got those hillbilly swine coming tomorrow to pick up this stuff. Don't go embarrassing me with all that hoopla."

Nick looks at Billy, fear beginning to show in his eyes as he begins piecing together the evidence before them. He opens his mouth to say something but shuts it quickly as the tirade from inside the shack continues.

"And you *will* continue putting on that getup every time we see someone too close to this operation or you'll be Bertha's next meal. You hear me? Just because we're kin won't change my mind, either. I'm not about to go back to the joint!"

Now the fear in Nick's eyes is real. Another piece of the puzzle has just fallen in place. "We got double trouble here, Billy," Nick whispers. "First off, these are the guys stealing all that stuff we read about in the paper. To make it worse, one of the guys is that escaped convict from Angola, Lufroy Aucoin."

"Yeah, it is," Billy replies quietly. "And it sounds like they're having someone come out tomorrow to pick up this stolen property."

"What do you think we should do?" Nick asks.

"Maybe we should pull the plug in their boat and then go back home to call the police."

"Yeah, that's probably about the smartest move," Nick says. "The police can be out here by morning and these guys won't be able to make a break for it."

Ever so quietly, the boys make their way to the boat that's bow is pulled up on the bank.

CHAPTER 7

Lufroy and Gator Bait

Gator Bait has never been in so much pain. It hadn't even hurt this bad when that mad mamma gator had grabbed him by the head after he tripped during his escape from her wrath for attempting to steal her eggs. Of course, Gator Bait had only been eight years old at the time, but he felt certain the pain hadn't been this bad. Now at thirty-eight years of age, two little boys had nearly blinded him with some potent concoction they'd sprayed at Rougarou's mouth, which just so happened to serve as his view port when wearing that darn costume. Now, huge blisters have formed around his eyes, covering a portion of the scar left over from the mad mamma gator's teeth. If only his cousin Lufroy wasn't so big. If he was as skinny as Gator Bait, then he could've been the one who fit in the costume. He was surely as mean as a real monster. Gator Bait's only a pretender, and monsters really scare him. He's even unnerved when he looks at his reflection in the mirror while wearing that Rougarou costume.

"It burns so bad, Lufroy," Gator Bait cries in a pathetic voice. "This willow bark tea isn't doing nothing."

"We're roughing it until we can get on our feet, Gator Bait," Lufroy responds. "Now, please quit that yammering. I swear, I never heard someone whine that much, even in prison." The two-hundred-fifty-pound, solid muscle bulk of Lufroy is at the gas burner heating them up some beans for supper. There isn't much room on the small table with the five security monitors lined up, but that's no problem. The peace that comes with added security is well worth the cramped quarters. Ever since Gator Bait had picked him up from the back of that truck stop after his escape from prison, he'd no choice but to listen to that crybaby moan about every little thing, whether he was hungry, tired, or hot, it didn't matter. His younger cousin had to tell him about every little discomfort he suffered. Although, he has to admit those blisters on Gator Bait's face do look mighty painful. But Lufroy'd never admit it.

Just make it until tomorrow, he silently tells himself for the hundredth time. *I'll have a pocket full of cash and I can abandon this idiot cousin for good.*

In prison, he'd met up with some cat with ties to the Hillbilly Mafia. He got pretty tight with this guy over the past three years and had even helped him out when some big lug had tried to force him to start paying for protection. When he told this appreciative hillbilly about his plan to escape while working on a road crew, he set in motion a plan that would help him get on his feet and on his way to Mexico. The plan was simple. Lufroy would steal enough boat motors, generators, and ATVs to fill a moving van and sell them to these Mountain Folk. The hillbillies liked this plan since these items are easy to sell and produce quite a nice profit. Lufroy was told to memorize a phone number and call it if he made it to freedom. Once free, and after he had located a secluded spot for his camp, he called the number to give them the coordinates of his location. His second call to them was to give them a list of the items he'd stolen. They'd insisted on knowing the year and condition of each item, then told him to call back the next day. When he'd called back, they informed him that they'd give him thirty thousand dollars. They also notified him of the day they'd arrive to pick up the stolen property.

His plan had been nearly flawless. After he'd hauled half of the stolen property that he currently had to this location, he noticed an old fella that lived nearby. This old guy was always snooping about, and on the day that he'd almost stumbled upon their loot, Lufroy decided he had to do something. He knew of a costume shop in a nearby town, as well as a home security business. He decided to break in to both places to get supplies and then rig the area with cameras to warn him of people who might get too close. At the costume store he intentionally stole a costume that would fit Gator Bait because most people who wandered around in the swamp had some type of weapon and he wasn't about to get *himself* shot. In the event that someone wandered too close, he'd have his cousin scare 'em away.

The Rougarou costume had done its job to perfection the first time. That old man hadn't run that fast since he was a teenager. And those two pesky boys had taken off just as fast when they saw the creature. If it weren't for one of them getting his foot caught up in something, Gator Bait wouldn't be sitting in the corner crying like a baby.

"Oh man, it hurts so bad," Gator Bait moans.

Lufroy doesn't even bother to holler back a reply. He lets his mind drift back to the virtual world he'd created while in prison—his only escape from the day-to-day boredom behind bars. In his daydream, he sees himself in Mexico, sitting on a beach and sipping umbrella drinks served by a pretty senorita. He knows there's no way he'd spend the rest of his life behind bars. His counselors in prison had told him to work on his anger issues and make the most out of his life behind bars. Those idiots couldn't understand that he'd done the world a favor by ridding it of that vermin, Whitey Broussard. And as far as *making the most of his life behind bars,* they could shove it.

After spending his first year in Angola, he'd decided that his best chance for escape was to earn a spot on the road crew. These guys left prison every morning to pick up trash along the highways. So, he just had to get on one of these work crews. Then once the crew transport van drove through the gates, the hardest part of his escape would be accomplished.

For the next year and a half he'd become a model prisoner. He'd obeyed all the orders from the guards without complaint and kept his temper under control when another inmate did something that angered him. These actions were noticed, and when he put in for a job transfer from the farm to the road crew, it was granted. He'd contacted the only relative dumb enough to help him and had him park in the back of a certain truck stop every day for several hours until Lufroy's road crew was ordered to pick up trash close by. The escape was much easier than he could have dreamed. He'd been studying the guard's habits since day one and learned that he spent half his time talking into a cell phone. As the crew was walking along the road in the vicinity of the truck stop, Lufroy had been patient and chose his moment carefully. The instant he saw the guard start waving his hands about as if he was talking to the person face-to-face, Lufroy had simply ducked off into the trees and made a dash for his cousin's old beat up pickup truck. As he ran he was thanking his lucky stars that the guard was a creature of habit, because if that phone call hadn't taken place, he wouldn't have made a break for it.

By the time the police had the area cordoned off, Lufroy and Gator Bait were twenty miles outside of the search zone and on their way to freedom.

Still in his dream world, Lufroy's being served his second umbrella drink by the same pretty senorita as always when his eye catches a movement on a monitor. His mind immediately rejoins his body as he focuses all of his attention on that monitor.

"Owww…"

"Hush up, Gator Bait! Somebody's out there," Lufroy retorts as he focuses on the movement he's spotted by the stolen boat he's been using. As he watches, he's barely able to see the outline of two bodies in the rear of the boat. If it weren't for the light bulb's reflection off of the boat's motor he never would have noticed the dark shape when it briefly blocked the reflection. Staring intently at the security monitor, he notices that the silhouettes he's seeing are about the same size as those two teenage boys that nearly blinded his cousin.

"I think our two boys are back," he whispers to his whimpering cousin while reaching in the corner for his shotgun.

"Let's get those little worms," Gator Bait responds.

After one more thoughtful look at the monitor to determine exactly where the shadows are located, Lufroy charges out the door and heads straight for the boat.

CHAPTER 8

The Chase

Hidden in shadows, Billy uses his fingers to feel around for the plug located somewhere on the lower half of the transom of the boat. When he finds it and pulls, the warm waters of Lost Bayou rush in over his fingers.

"Okay, I got it. Let's get back to your place and call the police."

"Yeah, I'm so ready to get out of here," whispers a very frightened Nick.

Just as Billy steps one foot out of the boat, the single door of the shack seems to explode outward as the huge frame of Lufroy charges out and heads straight at them. The sudden shock of the moment causes both boys to freeze.

Lufroy comes to a stop just ten feet from them. "You boys done did it now," he says. "Why you couldn't leave well enough alone when we chased you off last time?"

The boys remain silent and still, the fear from being caught by such a dangerous man causing paralysis.

"Gator Bait!" Lufroy shouts. "Come on out here!"

They can hear Gator Bait moaning inside the shack as he gets up off the floor. As he comes outside and stands beside his cousin, Gator Bait can't even form a smile on his face because of the pain. His eyes, however, glisten with joy as he confirms for himself that these are definitely the two that caused him the pain he's now suffering.

"Well, well, well, what do we have here? Looks to me like snack food for Bertha," Gator Bait says as he looks over at his cousin.

"Could be," says Lufroy. "Go get those pea-shooters, Gator Bait. And, you boys, don't try anything foolish."

The boys are stunned as they see what the bear spray has done to the skinny guy's face. Half of it is bubbled up with painful looking blisters that are so full they look ready to burst at any moment. Seeing this reminds Nick of the canister he stashed in his pocket. As Gator Bait steps forward to retrieve Billy's air rifle, Nick turns slightly to his side, reaching his hand into the pocket that is now out of sight of the two criminals. When it's Nick's turn to hand over his weapon, he waits for Gator Bait to step in front of Lufroy. Just as he extends his left arm to hand over his gun, he pulls his right hand out of his pocket and in one smooth motion brings it up while squeezing the trigger of the canister, hitting Gator Bait once again with a stream of repellent right in his face. He quickly twists his wrist causing the potent spray to rain down on Lufroy's head.

Both men instantly double over, screaming out curses and choking on the cloud of bear repellent engulfing them.

While Lufroy and Gator Bait are momentarily distracted— frantically trying to wipe the burning powder from their faces—Nick sees their chance. "Run, Billy!" he shouts.

These are wasted words since Billy was already on his way as the first hint of bear spray started hissing out of the canister. He's racing down the trail, visible now that the moon has made its way pretty high into the night sky.

Nick's action with the repellant was done so quickly, he didn't have time to concentrate a heavy dose at either man. It was just enough to blind them for the few seconds the boys need to make a break for it, and they've barely gone fifty feet along their way when they hear Lufroy shout at Gator Bait, "After them! They'll ruin everything if they get away!"

Intent on putting distance between themselves and the two criminals, the boys continue on their way at a fast and somewhat reckless pace. Suddenly, they see beams of light cutting across the trees in front of them. Now their predicament has just gotten worse.

"Don't slow down, Billy!" Nick shouts. "If they catch us we're in real trouble!"

Billy charges down the trail, jumping the log that had caused him to get stuck two days earlier. He hears a gator scurry into the water as he rushes along. He feels the thorns on the blackberry bushes ripping at his clothes and arms, but right now he doesn't care. Getting away is all that's on his mind.

As they come to the clearing of Mr. Pierre's home, he cuts toward the house, never slowing a bit. The gator is still there and doesn't budge as the two boys skirt the edges of the house and then veer back to the bayou to pick up the trail. They can now hear clearly the stomping and cussing of their pursuers not far behind, and then, suddenly, the sound of a blood-curdling scream followed by a shout from Gator Bait. "Bertha almost got me!"

They keep running, thankful that they haven't been tripped up or worse. The flashlight beam is still lighting the trees ahead of them, evidence that they're still being pursued. The light offers a brief glimpse of a tree leaning at head height across the trail and Billy is just barely able to duck his head in time to miss it. Just in the nick of time, he manages to give a warning to Nick, who ducks under the obstacle with hardly a slowdown in stride.

Billy spots the point where their trail comes out of the swamp and he slows just enough to take the turn. Now the water is knee deep and the dangers of tripping or twisting an ankle increase.

The boys can tell that their pursuers are only about a hundred feet behind them, so as they start through the water they slow down a little to minimize the sounds they're making...just in case they weren't spotted leaving the edge of the bayou. When the beam of light reaches the trail they've just taken into the swamp, it stops.

Looking back, Nick sees that Lufroy is manning the flashlight and hears him say, "They cut into the swamp somewhere in this area." Just then, the flashlight beam darts in their direction and holds the boys in its path. "There's the little ruffians!" Lufroy shouts. "Move it, Gator Bait!"

The boys begin running at a dangerous pace. Yet despite focusing their attention on speed rather than safety, just as their pursuers are doing, the boys are losing ground. It's not helping any that Lufroy and Gator Bait have the flashlight. Though the light helps the boys to see what's ahead, the bad guys are much bigger and stronger. It takes a lot of energy to push the water out of the way. The boys might be strong for their age but they're no match for the two grown men behind them.

The trunk of a cypress tree seems to explode beside Billy's head as Lufroy takes a shot in an effort to end this chase. With blood dripping from where the flying tree bark grazed his face, Billy cuts to the left to avoid the wasps' nest he knows is just ahead. After going around the nest and then returning to the trail, he's ready to surrender. He's breathing so hard and starting to get dizzy; the humidity coating his overworked lungs.

He's about to stop and hold up his hands, when a scream the likes of which he's never heard before, issues forth from Gator Bait, followed immediately by Lufroy's cursing.

"Keep going, Billy," Nick gasps breathlessly. "They found the wasps."

So he does, and though both boys are near total exhaustion, they need to take advantage of this fortunate mishap that's occurred in the chase.

Lying on his back in the water and using his flashlight, Lufroy can see that he's back paddled far enough from the nest to safely bring his head above the water. When his eyes break the surface, he sees his idiot cousin swinging his arms and screaming like a cat that's suddenly found itself in a room full of rocking chairs. "Hit the water, you fool!"

Immediately, Gator Bait does just that. Knowing his cousin will be able to hear him in this shallow water, Lufroy shouts, "Now move yourself underwater, away from the nest!"

A minute later, Gator Bait resurfaces and takes a deep breath. "They got me good, Lufroy!" he sputters. "I'm a dying. Oh my god, I hurt so bad."

Lufroy has no patience left. "I swear," he says as he stands up in the water, being careful to keep a tree between him and the nest. "I'll shoot you right now if you don't get up and help me catch those young'uns."

Fearing his cousin might do just that, Gator Bait stands up. The look on his face might have caused pity in Lufroy if pity was even possible. Gator Bait now has welts forming before his eyes. There are knots forming on any spot not occupied by blisters, and his grossly misshapen and lumpy head looks like nothing Lufroy has ever seen.

"Dang boy, you is a lot uglier than usual now. Come on, let's go catch those boys. I want them alive now so I can feed them to Bertha myself. Those wasps got me, too." And with that they both resume their pursuit.

Although Lufroy can no longer see the boys in the beam of his flashlight, he knows exactly which direction they took. All he has to do is follow the mud they kicked up in the clear swamp water. Lifting weights and doing hard labor in prison has made Lufroy rock-hard and Gator Bait can hardly keep up with the pace he's set. He knows the boys are worn out. He'd actually seen the leader of the two stop to surrender just before that first wasp had zapped him right on the forehead. He'll catch those two kids, that's a fact.

Billy is exhausted. He turns to Nick and sees that he's also about done. "I can't go no further, Nick."

"Let's just walk a bit to see if we can get our energy back," Nick suggests.

They slow their pace to a careful walking speed and, not even a minute later, they see the flashlight in the distance, right on the trail they'd just taken. As the crashing of powerful legs cutting through water reaches their ears, they look at each other, knowing the chase is all but over.

Just then Nick looks off to the side and spots what could be their only hope. "Look, Billy, a hollow log! We need to get up in there and hide."

Billy looks back at him with wide, terrified eyes. "You don't know what's in there, Nick."

"I know, but we don't have a choice," Nick states firmly. "Just follow me."

As the sounds of the chase get closer, Billy hands his friend the red flashlight he borrowed from his dad. "Here, use this."

Nick takes the flashlight and waits until he's bent down at the entrance of the trunk to turn it on. When he does he immediately spots, about two feet into the tree, three cottonmouths balled together. Quickly, he grabs a branch and, with no time to be scared, scrapes at the snakes until they're outside and swimming past his legs. He climbs into the hollow tree. Thankfully, there are no other unwelcome inhabitants inside. Billy follows him in and, once his feet are inside, lays motionless.

They listen in silence as the loud splashing gets closer. Just as the sound reaches the boys' hiding place, it stops. They can hear the deep breathing coming from the men standing near the log.

"Oh my god," Gator Bait whimpers. "I've never hurt so bad."

Lufroy has no sympathy for his cousin. "Relax cousin, this chase is over."

"Are we gonna let them go?" Gator Bait says, sounding relieved. "Can we just go back to the camp and go to bed?"

"Shut up, you fool!" shouts Lufroy. "Of course we ain't gonna let them go. We caught them." He looks down at the hollow log. "I see you boys trying to hide in that log. Now throw that demon spray out, then come out with your hands on your head or so help me I'm gonna start shooting from one end of that log to the other."

Hearing the sound of Lufroy's voice and his menacing threat, the boys immediately tense up.

"Hand the mace to me, Nick, so I can throw it out," Billy says. "We're caught."

Taking the canister from Nick, Billy throws it out through the opening in the log and they squirm their way out of the long-dead tree.

Only after both boys are back on their feet, and with their hands on their heads as directed, does Lufroy speak. "Gator Bait, go search their pockets for any other unpleasant surprises they might have in store for us. And I hope you're not such a big idiot that you don't remove those machetes from their belts first."

"It ain't that I'm a idiot if I'd a missed that Lufroy. I'm nearly blinded from that buzzard juice spray and those wasp stings." Gator Bait steps forward, obviously the loser of previous battles, but still trying to act tough. After he throws the machetes far off into the dark swamp, he roughly digs through the boys' pockets. Claiming a pocketknife from each of them, he pockets one and tosses the other to Lufroy. He also finds the red lensed flashlight on Nick and the compass on Billy, both of which he tosses to his cousin.

"Okay, they clean now, Lufroy."

"Now, boys, it seems like we at a point now where it's up to you if you want to be around to see the sun rise or not. Are we in agreement?"

Terrified and shaking, Billy and Nick nod their heads.

"Good. Now, what we're going to do is head back the way we came. If you try any funny stuff, I'll most certainly split you in half with this here scattergun. Do we have an understanding amongst ourselves?"

Once again, both boys nod their understanding.

"Fantastic. Here's your flashlight, boy. You and your friend lead the way back and we'll follow at a safe distance. Don't try to lead us into any more critter ambushes or I promise you that I *will* pull this trigger before I give in to anything that might come out at us. Is that understood as well?"

Nick nods his head and accepts the flashlight. He turns and starts heading back towards Mr. Pierre's place, with the red light eerily leading the way.

CHAPTER 9

Big Bertha

The walk back to the felon's hideaway is long, quiet, miserable, and terrifying. The night sounds have taken on a new and more frightening quality. The boys are in a life-threatening situation the likes of which neither has ever experienced. They're used to the expected dangers that exist in the swamp. Those are dangers they're prepared for and know how to handle. Being held captive by a convicted murderer and his dimwitted, disciple of a cousin is a dangerous and volatile situation they never expected.

As they come upon Mr. Pierre's place, Gator Bait apologizes to Big Bertha for not being able to feed her his leftovers, but promises that chances are good that she'll be getting a great feast later.

Hearing this Billy and Nick glance at each other worriedly.

"Shuddup, Gator Bait," Lufroy says.

The boys walk into the clearing at the hideout and are instructed to sit with their backs against the trunk of a tree. They end up sharing this particular tree with two of the stolen outboard motors.

Lufroy holds the gun on them while Gator Bait goes about tying them securely to the tree with a very course rope that bites painfully into their skin.

"What are we gonna do with them, Lufroy?" Gator Bait asks.

"I think we should hold on to them. At least until the hillbillies get here. Lord knows we ain't in no condition to load all this stuff on their boat."

"That's a good idea. My head hurts so bad I think it might explode. Can I go lay down?" Gator Bait pleads.

"Yeah, go lay down for a bit. I'll double check your knots and then grab that supper these boys so rudely interrupted." He sets his gun down and inspects his cousin's knot tying skills. "You might be a retard, but you sure can tie a knot," he says grudgingly.

"Thanks, Lufroy," Gator Bait replies, shocked by the only compliment he's ever received from his cousin. "I worked hard to learn them when I worked on that river tug." Then looking like the miserable lump of flesh he is, he heads inside to rest his aching body.

"Now boys, I've placed you here for a reason. The light bulb will give me more than enough light to see you with that camera right there." Lufroy points up at a camera the boys hadn't seen. "I'll have that monitor right by my side for the rest of the night. If I see either of you trying to make an escape, I'll come out and shoot you. Then I'll drag you out to the edge of the bayou where Bertha is. Do you understand?"

Both boys once again nod their understanding and Lufroy turns and heads inside.

Billy looks over at Nick who's already staring at him. "What are we gonna do, Nick?"

"I don't know. I guess we need to just keep from getting on their bad side and hope they let us go. If we do what they say, maybe they'll let us go after they've sold this stuff. They'll have their money. Hopefully, once that happens, they plan on leaving."

"This knot is tight," Billy whispers as he wiggles his wrists trying to loosen the rope. "I can't budge my hands. How about you?"

"No, I'm not going to be able to get loose. Let's just try to get through the night and see what happens tomorrow."

Though they try, neither Billy nor Nick is able to rest. They keep their faces buried between their knees to hide as best they can from the incessant mosquitoes buzzing around them. The sweat and swamp water has long since washed the repellant from their skin and they're now at the mercy of the hungry insects. To make things worse, their wrists are bloody from the futile attempts they've made to twist free. There's nothing to do now but suffer this situation as best they can.

After an hour, hundreds of welts from insect bites are visible on their arms and necks. Painfully, Nick lifts his head to look over at his friend. "I've never been so freaking miserable. I hope the mosquitoes leave enough blood for me to live."

"Don't worry, buddy." Billy lifts his head and looks at his friend. "They only need a drop each. You'll have plenty leftover. Just stay strong and we'll get through this."

At that moment they hear a deep, vibrating rumble coming from alongside the boat at the bayou's edge. The boys pale visibly. They know instantly what's making that sound...the deeper the rumble, the bigger the gator. And *this is one deep rumble.* Snapping their heads in the direction of the water, they see the red reflection of the gator's eyes, a common occurrence when light hits its eyes in the dark of night.

As they watch it, they can see that it's watching them from about ten feet out into the bayou.

"That looks like Bertha," Nick whispers softly. "She must've gotten tired of waiting for Gator Bait to feed her."

"That's not good," a worried Billy manages to respond.

Having spent so much time in the swamp, they both know that most gator attacks are usually the fault of humans. Normally, gators are very leery of humans and tend to give humans a wide berth. But once people feed them, the gators come to see the humans as a source of food and their shyness goes away. Usually, it's tourists that feed them, not realizing that by doing so they're creating a danger for the people who call this place home and spend their leisure time on the water. Unfortunately, once it's known that a gator's been fed by humans, it needs to be put down before it can attack someone.

Bertha's gotten so big because she's got this secluded section of the bayou, far removed from the tour boats, all to herself. The only human she's probably ever seen is Mr. Pierre and he'd know better than to feed her. Then along came Gator Bait.

As they watch, it's apparent that the gator is slowly making its way to shore. "We need to wake them up or that thing's gonna get us for sure," Nick says.

"Lufroy! Gator Bait! Get out here!" Billy shouts.

Unfortunately, Billy's shouts seem to sound like a wounded animal to Big Bertha. First, she rests her head on the bank. Then, she uses her immensely powerful leg muscles to lift her body and take a cautious step onto land.

Now it's Nick's turn to holler. "Get out here, please! There's a gator gonna get us!"

Bertha takes another step forward, looking at them through cold, emotionless, reptilian eyes. Her tough hide glistens as the droplets of water resting on it reflect from the light of the single bulb. The boys can see a plume of mist billow from her nostrils as she exhales. They start to squirm, digging the rope deeper into their wrists as they try to break free—their pleas for help unanswered.

Sensing no danger from this potential meal, Bertha suddenly takes three steps forward. The hungry gator is now only ten feet away.

"Please, help us!" the boys scream in unison.

After a couple more awkward but powerful steps, Bertha is just five feet from the boys. Panic overtakes them and they start screaming and kicking their feet in a futile attempt to keep the predator at bay.

Bertha takes another cautious step—three feet away now. She's reached a gator's preferred distance for making its final lunge. But, this gator is old and cautious. Had she been a younger, less experienced gator, the boys would already be in pain.

She's made up her mind that there are no dangers presented by this meal, so she decides to grab hold of the foot closest to her mouth—the foot of the shorter, meatier looking prey.

Suddenly, a crater forms in the ground six inches in front of the gator's snout as the loud boom of a shotgun blast silences all other noise. Bertha immediately spins her immense bulk, and using a speed not thought possible for such a large animal, runs for the bayou. She slides off the muddy bank and into the dark water with hardly a ripple.

A burst of laughter replaces the silence created by the shotgun blast. "That was the most fun I had in years," Lufroy says, doubling over with laughter. "You boys thought you was done for, didn't you?"

"Thank you, sir," Nick sputters, tears streaming from his eyes. "You saved us."

"Sir? *Sir?* Well that's a first. It wasn't because of the kindness in my heart that I did it," Lufroy states so there's no mistaking his meanness. "I still need you to help load this stuff on the boat later this morning."

Now standing beside Lufroy, Gator Bait, with his lumpy, misshapen head, just has to put in his two cents. "I wanted to feed Bertha. You're lucky my cousin was here and scared it away."

"Shuddup, Gator Bait," Lufroy replies predictably. "You talk mean but we both know that you don't have the kind of meanness in you that I do. Tell them the truth. While we were watching on the monitor you practically begged me to come outside and rescue them."

The feeling of enjoyment he gets from belittling his cousin washes over him. "It'll be daylight soon and that's when the hillbillies told me they'd get here. Personally, I don't think they're smart enough to find the coordinates I gave them so they'll probably be late. Go ahead and pack our clothes, Gator Bait. I want to get out of here as soon as I'm paid. Boys, you just stay calm and you might just be home by this afternoon, telling your parents about your little adventure."

The boys were just beginning to shake off the trauma they'd been subjected to and their tears had stopped but their cheeks are now stained with streaks of mud. Neither one of them had really believed they'd be set free, but Lufroy's latest statement has rekindled hope in their bellies.

"Please, sir," Billy pleads, "our word is good. We won't say anything to anyone. Just let us go after we help you."

"I'm done putting trust in people's words, boy. You'll feel the same way when you get to my age. I'll let your behavior judge your outcome. I'm not a child killer and don't want to become one, but I will if you give me a reason. By the time you make it home, we'll be long gone so I'm not worried about that."

Lufroy turns away and begins looking for the things lying around that he and Gator Bait will be taking with them. Nick looks at Billy. "I don't trust that guy one bit. He's a no good thief and killer who can't even show his cousin any respect. Why should he be truthful to us?"

"I feel the same," Billy replies. "We have to keep our eyes open for any chance we might have to get away. That cousin of his is in no shape to keep up with us. But that Lufroy knows a little something about the swamp. He's the one that will definitely be able to catch us."

The boys grow quiet as they listen to the sound of an approaching boat. "Okay, Billy," Nick breaks their brief silence, "when those hillbillies get here just do as you're told. Do you see that cypress tree growing out of the water on the other side of the bayou?"

Looking in the direction of the bayou, Billy spots the tree about twenty feet from their side of the bayou and five feet from the opposite bank. "Yeah, I see it."

Nick explains to him the plan he's come up with that offers them the best chance of escape. "If it looks like our lives are in danger then you hightail it and jump in. I think if we can swim underwater to that tree, we can come up on the other side and keep the tree between them and us as we take off into the swamp. Lufroy will definitely chase us, so we gotta move as fast as we can."

"Let's just hope it doesn't come to that." As Billy finishes saying what they're both thinking, the approaching boat comes into view further down the bayou.

CHAPTER 10

The Hillbilly Mafia

"I see three of them, Lufroy," says Gator Bait, as the two of them emerge from the camp carrying a couple of canvas bags stuffed with their clothes.

"I ain't blind, you idiot," retorts Lufroy. "They sure don't look like what I thought a hillbilly'd look like. These boys are big."

"I hope they don't expect me to help with anything. My head feels like there's a weasel in it digging through my brain," Gator Bait whines.

His cousin looks at him like he's ready to punch him in the nose to show him what real pain feels like. "You're gonna do whatever it is me or these fellas tell you to do. And if you cry about your infirmities just once while they're here, I'll whoop you silly when they leave." Lufroy looks over at his captives. "Cut them boys loose so the hillbillies don't see that they're our prisoners. And boys, you're my nephews come out to make a few dollars helping us load. You got it?"

Both boys nod their understanding as Gator Bait bends down and, using Billy's knife, quickly cuts through the rope.

They approach the bayou's edge as the three men from Arkansas run the bow of their boat up onto the bank. Whatever Lufroy might have thought of this bunch before, he has to admire their choice of boat for this operation. It's a flatboat at least thirty feet long and a good ten feet wide. The center console is only taking up a small six-foot area on the stern end of the vessel. Located directly behind the captain's seat are two powerful 250 horsepower Yamahas that can effortlessly and speedily bring this boat and its cargo anywhere they want it taken. What's most impressive, though, is the twenty feet of cargo space located in front of the driver's console.

The men have even thought enough in advance to bring a heavy-duty wheelbarrow and ramp attachment for the bow, to make loading easier. This is a much better planned operation than Lufroy thought possible from a group of no-good hillbillies who think they're mafia material.

Immediately after the boat comes to a stop, one of the trio marches across the deck and slides the ramp out onto the bank. He lifts the angled end of it into a slot cut into the boat's deck. With the ramp now in place, he turns around without saying a word, and walks back across the deck to stand beside the immense bulk of a man sitting in the copilot's chair. He's so big that his butt cheeks are actually hanging a foot down on both sides of the seat.

Lufroy breaks the uncomfortable silence. "How you fellas doing? I got your goods right over here. Whatcha say we get you loaded up so we can be done with it."

All three men in the boat just stare for a solid minute at the man on shore. "My name's Roscoe Clinton and you will *never* call me *fella* again," the big man in the copilot's seat says. "You call me Mr. Clinton, or sir." He motions to the man next to him sitting in the captain's chair. "This is my son, Jed, and the gentleman who lowered the ramp is my most trusted soldier, Jasper. How about slowing things down just a bit and introduce me to your crew. I like to know who I'm doing business with. I'm assuming you're Lufroy."

One thing Lufroy had learned in prison was how to spot the men you don't mess with, and this man was one of them. "My apologies, sir, I meant no disrespect. Yes, I'm Lufroy. This here is my cousin, Gator Bait. He got that scar from a gator when he was a little boy. These two young fellas here are my nephews Todd and T-Roy. They come out to earn a few dollars."

Roscoe looks over at Gator Bait. "What's wrong with your face?" he asks. "Not the scar, I mean the blisters. Your cousin here burn you?"

Gator Bait is instantly confused, which causes the panic he's been experiencing to clearly show on his face. He simply isn't bright enough to come up with a good lie all on his own at a moment's notice. He looks at Lufroy, his eyes begging for a little help. Lufroy just stares back with a blank expression on his face. His eyes, however, promise a lot of unpleasantness if he should tell the truth. So Gator Bait decides to just keep his mouth shut like his cousin warned him to do.

"What's the matter with you? Cat got your tongue?" Roscoe asks.

Lufroy speaks for Gator Bait. "You have to forgive my cousin. He's not the brightest and gets tongue-tied when speaking to strangers. Truth is, he tripped on a stump while he was carrying a pot of hot beans. They splattered all over his face and it burnt…"

"Shut your trap, you lying vermin." Roscoe's sharp command instantly halts whatever else Lufroy is about to say. "What do you take us for? Do you think we run some kind of backwoods operation here? Six hours after you sent me the coordinates of your camp, I had Jasper and three of his men watching you from across this here creek. Jasper and his crew are ex-Army Rangers. You never saw them…but they saw everything you did. I started off admiring the way you secured your camp. I even got a laugh out of the report I received of you scaring the old man and your *nephews* away with that there werewolf costume."

For the first time since he'd been sentenced to life in prison, Lufroy is afraid. These guys are much more organized than he thought possible. They're definitely made of mafia material. "I-I-I'm sorry, sir. We did—"

"Shut up! I told you to keep your lying chatterbox closed, didn't I? Don't say a word until I'm done! I had Jasper stick around to see if your little monster costume worked. It seemed to have done just that. Until Jasper called me directly when he seen them boys creeping up to your camp the second time. I gave him instructions to shoot you both if the boys had gotten away. You're lucky Jasper isn't lazy. Instead of just shooting you the instant you got hit with the mace for the second time, like I would have done, he gave you the opportunity to give chase and make the capture. He had you lined up in his night scope and was going to put a bullet in you if you'd run past that log the boys were hiding in."

To emphasize the point Roscoe's making, Jasper reaches behind his console and produces a very powerful looking rifle, which he levels at Lufroy.

"Not just yet, Jasper, let me finish," instructs his boss. "Lufroy, contrary to what you think of me and my hillbilly clan—yes, I got a report on your personal feelings directed our way—we are a tight family. Our business is professionally run and we have ties higher up the ladder than you'll ever know. Every decision I make is based on how it will help my kin. I also reward those that help me." To emphasize his daddy's point, Jed nods his head as if no truer words were ever spoken.

"I believe you know Ned Ferguson, my nephew. He's not the brightest boy and he proved that when he decided to do some business on his own outside of our beloved state of Arkansas, and got caught. But he's family, just the same. He told me how you had his back in a couple of bad situations down there in that prison. Only because of that, I ain't gonna have you shot right now. I'll keep my promise to him by helping you get on your feet."

Full of fear, Lufroy mumbles a near silent thanks.

"What I can't overlook," Roscoe continues, "is the disrespect you show not only to my kin but to your own. There's no excuse for the rudeness you show that cousin of yours. So I'm gonna teach you the manners your pappy should'a taught you long ago. I'm gonna pay you fifteen thousand dollars—half of what was agreed upon. If you don't like that, we'll just take your stuff and leave you with nothing. How does that sit with you?"

Lufroy's temper is about to boil over, but he's not stupid enough to let his anger show. Even an ill-tempered, lawless dog like himself has self-preservation built into his DNA. "Yes sir," he answers his face red with anger, "that seems more than fair."

"Glad we have an understanding." The big man looks at the group standing beside Lufroy. "Gator Bait, boys, you all've had a bad night. Why don't you go sit in the shade by that tree over yonder? And you," he says, directing his gaze once again on Lufroy, "get on up here and grab this wheelbarrow. You got some work to do."

CHAPTER 11

Lufroy's Anger Rises

Lufroy is sweating like a hog, keeping silent as he makes one haul after another onto the deck of the boat. His red face and dark stares, continuously returning to the three sitting under the tree, give away his promises of wrath to be let loose on them in the near future. The mafia boss, his son, and soldier remain on the boat, watchful of any problems that might arise from the hotheaded brute as he works to load the boat.

Sitting in the hot, humid shade Gator Bait is finally succumbing to the exhaustion overtaking his body. He's in a bad way and his body is working hard to heal itself. Even the fear he felt every time his cousin looked his way is not enough to keep his eyelids open. What began with his head snapping upright every few seconds as he fought to stay awake, has ended with his head dropping to his chest, followed almost instantly by the sound of a light snore.

"We don't stand a chance if we make a run for it, now," Nick whispers, looking over at Billy. "That guy with the gun has us covered no matter what direction we run."

"Yeah, I've noticed that, but we gotta at least try, don't we?"

"We need to keep our eyes open. I don't see anything we can do right now without getting hurt, so let's just stay calm and wait it out," Nick instructs.

Jed Clinton, Roscoe's son is thirty-five years old and 250 pounds. It's obvious that he's still powerful but it doesn't take a genius to see that much of his muscle is turning to fat and that he'll be just like his father in another ten years. He's been silent since they pulled up but his irritation at sitting so long in this infernal heat and humidity is making him impatient. "What in tarnation is taking you so long? Get a move on it, why don't ya?"

"Quiet, boy," his father instantly reprimands. "Ain't I taught you better than to criticize a man while he's working and you're sitting on your tush? If'n you want things to speed up get off this boat and give the feller a hand."

This instantly causes Jeb to shut his mouth. He knows that there's no way he could get out there and work in this humidity without getting heat stroke. "Sorry, Paw, I'm just ready to get this over with so I can get back to my Marcy-May. She's been having a real tough time with this pregnancy."

"You gotta learn that when it's time for business you keep your mind on the here and now or you'll find yourself in a bad predicament," his father advises.

Jed isn't about to let his father know that his own discomforts are the cause of the comment he made—not his wife's difficulties caused from being pregnant with twins. His paw doesn't like weak men. A shiver passes through him as he recalls some of the examples his father has made of lazy or unreliable help he's hired in the past.

"You just keep doing like you're doing, Lufroy. Here, take a break and drink some water before you pass out," Roscoe says as he tosses a bottle of ice-cold water over to the worn out laborer.

Without a word, Lufroy snatches the bottle midair and downs its contents. Instantly, he gets back to work. He just wants to be done with this whole business so he never has to see these swine again. He would've already made an excuse to enter the shack to retrieve his gun and shoot all three of these hillbillies, but he knows those Army compadres of Jasper's are still unaccounted for, hiding out there somewhere. He can practically feel the sights of their guns aimed at his body.

Once he's been paid and the hillbillies leave, he's gonna make those pesky brats wish they'd never let their curiosity get the best of them. If it weren't for them, there would have been no reason to lie. If there was no lie, then Roscoe would have admired the security system he'd installed and the way he went about scaring away intruders. But these two little boys have made him look like a fool. And far worse is that they've cost him fifteen grand. Oh yes, they would pay dearly.

After an hour or so of loading the boat, Lufroy is nearly done. As he listens to Gator Bait's quiet snores, Nick looks at Billy. "He's only got three motors left to load but look how he's slowed down," he whispers. "The heat is getting to him. We need to make our move as soon as the hillbillies leave—before he has time to rest."

"I agree. I just hope that Roscoe don't see us as a threat."

Five minutes later, Lufroy struggles to lift the final outboard motor out of the wheelbarrow and set it on the deck. He immediately drops to his knee as a wave of dizziness sweeps over him. He grabs the boat's railing to keep from falling over.

"He don't have long before he passes out if he don't sit in the shade and drink some water," Nick whispers.

Seeing that Lufroy isn't doing well, Roscoe hands him another bottle of water, which Lufroy opens and begins to drink. When the bottle is half empty, Lufroy swings his head over the side of the boat and hurls the contents of his stomach into Lost Bayou.

"It looks like you better go sit down and rest a spell in the shade, Lufroy," Roscoe advises. "You'll need to recuperate before you get that boat of yours bailed out. And it seems to me that you're the only one of your bunch strong enough to pull that heavy boat far enough out of the water to start bailing."

From his perch on the flatboat, Lufroy looks over at his own boat and notices for the first time that the rear end is completely submerged. Bailing will do no good unless the upper portion of the entire boat is above the water level. He knows he's the only one strong enough to pull the boat up onto the bank, but he's also aware that it'll be impossible for him to do in his current condition.

He looks over at the boys with murder in his eyes. "You boys will pay dearly for that," he warns. "I know this had to be your doing last night when I caught you over here next to it."

"Now, now, Lufroy," cautions Roscoe. "Nothing will happen to those boys in my sight. I would never hurt a child who follows his natural curiosities. Once we make it back into the hills we'll be safe from any kind of law. You, on the other hand, had best get going quick to where ever it is you're going. Those boys aren't any threat to me and if you had planned this operation out through its entirety, you wouldn't have anything to worry about either."

The boys breathe a sigh of relief. They trust the words of this hillbilly more than they do Lufroy's. There's still a chance for them to get out of the mess they've found themselves in.

"Jasper, contact your men and tell them to start making their way back to the spot on the bayou where we picked you up," Roscoe instructs his soldier, who produces a radio from his pocket and passes on the instructions. "Lufroy, come over here and get your money."

Lufroy gets up and on weak, unsteady legs, walks over to the rear of the boat. He's handed a thick envelope, and a quick glance inside offers him a glimpse of a stack of Ben Franklins. Finally, his ticket to a new life!

"Ned wanted me to tell you that he wishes you luck," Roscoe says. "I suppose he's forced to consort with the likes of you while he's locked up, but I'll still warn him that he had best forget any bad habits he might have learned in there before he comes home."

Lufroy just eyes him for a moment. "Thank you, sir," he manages to say, purely out of the fear he feels when talking to this imposing figure. Turning around, he pulls the ramp back onto the boat.

"Okay, boy, back this thing up," Roscoe instructs Jed once Lufroy has jumped off the boat. "Our business is finished here."

And with that the motors crank up. Jed needs to give it full throttle in reverse to get the heavily laden vessel to slide back off of the bank. Once he's aligned the boat in the middle of the bayou, he shifts it into forward and they begin making their way back the way they had come.

As soon as the boat is underway, Lufroy opens the envelope and starts counting the bills. Satisfied that he hasn't been cheated, he turns his attention to the three sitting under the tree.

"Wake up, you idiot!"

Gator Bait, who's been dreaming of a nice picnic lunch with Lucinda, the only girlfriend he's ever had, and a girl who only exists in his mind, is jarred instantly awake by the sharp command. He brings his eyes up to bear on the only other set of eyes that scare him more than that momma gator's did so many years before. He's slept through most of the loading process so he missed much of the warning signs that a firestorm of wrath was building in his cousin.

"The hillbillies are gone already?" he asks, looking around.

That's all it takes to set Lufroy off. Waving his arms like a mad man he storms off in the direction of the three figures clustered together in the shade of the tree.

CHAPTER 12

The Mad Dash

Lufroy grabs Gator Bait by the collar of his shirt and jerks him to his feet so fast that his head whips back and slams into the trunk of the tree he'd been resting against. Gator Bait begins to scream like a little boy. Suddenly, Lufroy draws his hand back and slaps him across the face so hard that all the blisters on the left side of Gator Bait's face explode—just like those little ketchup packages when you stomp down on them in the parking lot of a fast food restaurant. Gator Bait's flung down to the ground near the entrance of the trail heading to Mr. Pierre's place, and he begins whimpering loudly.

Lufroy's anger has now taken full control of his body. As he directs his attention to scolding his cousin, Nick grabs Billy's arm. "Follow me," he whispers.

Nick leads the way alongside the raggedy shack and heads straight out into the swamp, each step carefully placed to avoid splashing the water or tripping on hidden obstacles. About two hundred feet into their mad dash, they hear Lufroy's shouts. "Where did they go? Get up, Gator Bait! We gotta find them!"

The boys continue their careful pace—trying to keep any noise from giving them away. Suddenly, they hear loud, violent splashing behind them and more shouting. "There they are! Get a move on it, Gator Bait!"

"Run, Nick!" Billy screams, as he pulls ahead of his friend in a natural response to take the lead. They have a good lead, but judging by the sounds of splashing behind them, that lead is shrinking by the second.

Nick's a very quick thinker in stressful situations. He's proven this by the quick, instinctive actions he's often taken at critical moments in competitive sports. It's obvious to every spectator who watches him compete that he has a gift. Fortunately for the boys, Nick's gift doesn't kick in only in non-life threatening endeavors, and as he runs, he's taking in all of his surroundings—searching for an advantage to present itself.

The first thing his unique brain realizes is the fact that this area of the swamp differs in one big way from the trail they cut from Swamp Camp to Lost Bayou. When cutting that trail, they were in an area of the swamp that had more trees, offering better coverage. That was good in one obvious way—the thicker trees provided more obstructions to direct line of sight. However, in that thicker cover, the water was clear, which allowed the path they took to easily be tracked by the mud they disturbed as they made their way through.

By being forced to take this new route directly from the criminals' hideout, they find themselves traveling in an area of the swamp where the trees are spaced farther apart, allowing more sunlight to shine through. This is bad news when it comes to escaping a tracker's view, but because of his quick thinking, Nick has spotted two inhabitants of the swamp that hadn't existed along the trail they tried to escape on the night before. Had they existed on that trail, the boys might have been able to dodge capture.

The two inhabitants that just might offer aid in the boys' escape are not animals, but plants.

The first of which is duckweed. These very small plants resemble lily pads, but are only half the size of a contact lens. The little green fronds have an air pocket that allows them to float on the surface and the additional sunlight caused by the increased distance between trees has allowed them to flourish. Unknown to many people is the fact that this plant is higher in protein than a soybean, which is the reason it's a main staple for foraging waterfowl. Some people in Southeast Asia actually make it a part of their diet. Though, right now, Nick isn't thinking of food. He's thinking of the fact that these small pads clustered tightly together, and offering no visibility below them, have no roots. This will offer the boys a place of concealment and movement if needed.

However, this concealment will be *under water*, which could be a predicament. Fortunately, Nick has also spotted the perfect plant to partner with the duckweed in resolving this issue, and as the boys continue kicking water out of their way in this life or death struggle to escape, Nick tells Billy to pull up—by its roots—the next big water lily he passes. After gulping in a fresh breath of hot, humid air, he instructs him to break the root end off, but to leave the leaves on.

His choice for improving their chances at going undetected beneath the duckweed is perfect. The water lily is a plant that has adapted well to survive in water with little oxygen. Its leaf stem is hollow, allowing the roots buried deep in the mud to breathe. Also, known by few, is the fact that the American Indians once pounded the dried roots of this plant into flour, which they then baked into pancakes. Nick knows there's also a medicinal use for the plant, but at the moment he can't seem to recall what it is.

The water lilies are scattered about every twenty yards or so. "Okay, Billy," Nick says when they've each got a lily stem in their grasp, "he's still catching up with us. When we get past that little thicket of vines up ahead, we're going to get down into the water. The duckweed will hide us and you can breathe through the stem. Just be careful not to move it."

"I sure hope this works," Billy says without slowing down. "If it doesn't, then we're done for."

As they near the tangle of vine growth, Billy risks a look back hoping that Lufroy has slowed down in his nearly exhausted state. Unfortunately, the fear of them escaping has allowed their pursuer to dig deep for some extra energy and he's still charging strong as Billy loses sight of him through the vines.

"Quick! Lay down next to that log over there," Nick instructs. He knows from instinct that most people won't come closer than just a few feet to a solitary log lying in the swamp, simply because it's a magnet for certain unsavory, slithering reptiles.

Without a word, Billy sits down next to the log and places his nature-made snorkel in his mouth. The fat cottonmouth, stretching out on the log in the sun, doesn't even cause a pause as Billy lies back in the water.

Nick, who decided to face the opposite direction so that their feet can remain in contact, is relieved to see the duckweed instantly cover the spot where his friend's face should be. He places the lily stem in his mouth and leans back, allowing the warm embrace of swamp water to cover, and then hide, his face.

Once underwater, Nick opens his eyes and sees that he is indeed contained in the shadows of the wild aquatic plant. Although the water is warm, the shadows he hides in are much more comfortable than the blazing sun above the water's surface. Another pleasant surprise is the fact that his breathing is coming easily through the lily's stem. He sees that his nose is only inches below the surface, and it worries him a little that he's able to see above the surface, through the small gaps that have formed between the plants. Remembering how his friend was totally camouflaged does bring him some relief, though, and he realizes it's the same effect as looking into a room—looking *from* a lit room into the shadows is more difficult than looking *into* a lit room from the shadows.

Nick's surprised that he can hear so well under the shallow water and Lufroy's loud crashing through the water is clearly audible. As the crashing nears, he's made aware of Billy's ability to hear as well because he feels his friend's foot pushing harder against his own.

Billy's concentrating totally on not moving his breathing tube. He hears Lufroy's approach and tenses. He comforts himself by pushing his foot against his friend's a little tighter. This is another good idea his friend thought of. Without the constant contact, Billy might very well have succumbed to the feeling of being alone out here and panicked. As he takes in a slow breath, tainted with the flavor of vegetation, he wills his nerves to remain calm. He focuses on the good things. His first thought being that they now stand a chance of making it home and how Hanna's long brown hair and smiling eyes directed his way are all he wants to see again. He decides that if he can make it through this, then there's no way he'll be too shy to ask her out on a date. If she only knew how often she was on his mind. His thoughts continue to drift and he visualizes his father squatting in an awkward position as he makes a weld at work, unaware of his son's trouble. He realizes then that the mosquito bites from the night before are no longer itching. This in itself is enough to celebrate. He had scratched himself raw while sitting under that tree watching Lufroy load that boat. Thoughts of Lufroy quickly bring him back to the present. He hears the man getting very close, then... nothing.

While Lufroy is charging through the water to catch the boys, his mind has gone mad with anger. He's forgotten all about his exhaustion—all he's thinking of is catching these bothersome brats and snapping their necks as soon as he gets his hands on them. There will be no more taking prisoners. That was a mistake the first time.

That worthless cousin of his is nowhere in sight. Most likely, he's still lying on the ground back there, crying like a baby. Once he's done with the boys, he'll return to finish his cousin off and drag him out to where the boys were—never to be found. Lufroy'd be home free at that point. The boys' disappearance could never be tied to him and, because of that, the law would have no new clues to point them in his direction. But first, he had to catch those two kids.

As he rounds a tangle of vines that are growing upward into the upper branches of a cypress tree, he realizes that he can't see where the boys have gone and stops in his tracks. Methodically, he scans the swamp ahead of him with his eyes, while listening intently. The trees are spaced far enough apart to have made it impossible for them to run so far ahead to no longer be visible. And since he'd been gaining on them the whole time, that brief thirty seconds of not being able to see them should've ended with them coming into view even closer. That leaves only one logical answer, they're hiding.

Lufroy stands there a moment to allow the sudden wave of dizziness that has snuck up on him to pass. He notices that goose bumps have formed on his arms; he's definitely suffering from heat exhaustion. In order to keep it from progressing to heat stroke, he needs to sit down and cool off as much as possible. If he becomes unconscious out here, he'll fall into the water and drown. It's good that the boys are hiding. It'll give him a chance to bring his temperature back down and keep his eyes open for them at the same time.

Looking around for a place to rest, he spots the nearest thing that'll serve as a seat, a log resting on its side, one end in the shade, about twenty feet in front of him.

As Lufroy approaches the log he spots a cottonmouth, about two feet long, relaxing in the afternoon sun. He wants to sit in the shady spot, a few feet from the snake, but he's not about to share his space with this critter. So, breaking off a rotten branch from the log, he uses it to slide the snake into the water, just opposite from where he plans to rest.

CHAPTER 13

The Long Soak

Billy has been focusing most of his senses on locating Lufroy's location since he stopped the splashing. Surprisingly, this underwater world he finds himself submerged in is far from silent. He's not sure what he's hearing but suspects that the different clicks and clacks are from creatures quietly communicating with one another just like their distant cousins do above the surface.

Billy feels the log he's resting against shift slightly, and hears the loud crack of a branch being broken off. He watches Lufroy's shadow above the surface as it moves on the other side of the log, all the while hoping that Lufroy doesn't use the branch he just broke off as a club to pound him and Nick. Suddenly he feels a weight land on his lap, knowing instantly that it's the snake he saw resting above him just before he laid back in the water. Billy can feel the wiggling movement as the snake swims up his body, and he stares up, wide-eyed, as its lower jaw stops right above his eyes! Using the same strategy as the boys' to conceal itself, the snake is submerged and, obviously, it thinks it's resting on a log. But, the problem is that the snake's body is resting on *Billy's* chin, neck, and chest and it takes every bit of his self-control to remain motionless and not gulp in a lung full of water. All he can do is watch as the snake scrutinizes the strange creature above that has disturbed its rest. Fortunately for Billy, the snake is more cautious than curious and it decides to make a slow retreat deeper into the safety of the swamp. As he watches the snake slither over his face, Billy breathes a deep sigh of relief through the stem of the water lily and once again counts his blessings.

Nick's lying there motionless as well. He, too, feels the log move and hears the branch break. He hears the splash in Billy's direction and feels, through the contact he has with his foot, his friend's body stiffen. He knows what's just happened. *Hang in there, buddy,* he thinks to himself. *That snake don't know you're down here. He just wants to get away.*

Nick feels better once he feels Billy's foot relax a bit. He watches as Lufroy's shadow moves to the shady end of the log, and confirming his fears, there's a very subtle roll of the log—Lufroy has chosen *this* log as a resting place from which to stake out the area. He must've figured out that the boys were hiding and decided to wait them out.

The good thing is that Lufroy probably suspects the boys are hiding behind a tree, and because the trees are spaced so far apart, he must think they'll become visible once they poke their heads out or try to move from one tree to the next.

The bad thing is that Lufroy is resting up. Nick knows that once that man's body has rested, he and Billy won't stand a chance if they're spotted.

Another thing that Nick has been pondering is the time; it's got to be at least noon by now. His mom'll be expecting him to show up at any moment. It won't be much longer before she'll become worried and get in touch with Billy's mom. Hopefully, once they get together they'll work each other into a tizzy and demand a search party be sent out. Even if this happens he knows that it'll be hours before anyone goes to look for them at Swamp Camp. And even if they do there's no way they'll be able to guess which direction to start searching. Nick isn't even sure where they are. For the first time he realizes that he and Billy are lost out here and getting away from Lufroy is but the first trial they face.

Lufroy sits on the log, motionless and silent. He's looked at every tree within two hundred feet at least ten times. He thought he'd spotted one of them once, but it ended up being a squirrel coming around the trunk of a tree, seeming to want to play a game of peek-a-boo. After it had peeked out at him a third time, Lufroy realized that it wasn't human and got so mad that he would have shot it if he hadn't rushed off without his gun.

The dizzy spells have long since ceased, along with the chills and goosebumps, and after several hours of sitting here, Lufroy's beginning to think that the boys might not be around after all. He decides to speak out anyway. "Okay, boys. I know you're out there somewhere. Why don't you come on out so we can go back to the camp and talk about this over a nice cold bottle of water." He sits quietly for a moment, listening to his surroundings and staring out over the swamp. "Y'all know I can't take the chance of you getting back home and calling the police before I get out of here. What I'll do is tie you up just tight enough to hold you a bit. All I need is a little head start and you'll never see me again. In two days I'll be sipping drinks on a beach in Mexico, a thousand miles from here."

The longer his deceitful offer goes unanswered the angrier he becomes. He can feel it in his bones that they heard every word he said. "Okay boys, this is your last chance! I'm about to start searching behind every tree you could have possibly reached while you were out of my sight. And if you make me go through all that trouble, I'll strangle you both when I get my hands on ya."

He gets to his feet and walks around the log, heading for the nearest tree. He decides to walk back and forth from one tree to the next in a pattern that doesn't extend out past what was invisible to him as he approached the cluster of vines. As he zig zags back and forth from one tree to the next, the distance to what he searches for steadily grows.

Nick hears Lufroy's splashes getting farther away. He figures that this might be a good opportunity to move a little farther out of the villains search area. He slowly lifts his head, careful to not let the end of his lily stem become submerged. He wipes the tiny vegetation from his eyes with the one finger that he raises above the surface. Even with the upper half of his face above the water's surface, it's difficult to make him out. The tiny plants that have concealed him so well now cling to his face, helping him to blend in completely with his surroundings.

He sees Lufroy marching from one tree to the next. He's about a hundred feet out and getting farther away as he continues to work the search pattern that he's chosen.

Nick taps Billy's foot three times with his own and watches the duckweed over his friend's face slowly form a mound. Two wide eyes become visible as Billy uses a finger the same way Nick had to clear away the clinging vegetation. "Let's scoot our butts along the bottom and try to put some distance between us and this log."

His friend nods in agreement and Nick begins slowly making his way along the length of the log in the direction of the shade where Lufroy had chosen to stand sentry. They remain on their backs, creeping backwards on their elbows. With only their camouflaged faces above the surface they're as good as invisible.

The boys can see Lufroy off to their right moving from one tree to the next. When he's between trees looking around in an unpredictable manner, the boys stop all movement. Several times his eyes sweep across the boys' but he doesn't hesitate as though a curiosity has caught his eye.

After a half hour of moving at a snail's pace, the boys are outside of the search pattern by fifty feet or so—a good seventy-five feet from the log where they'd started. This is when they hear Lufroy stomping back towards his starting point. He's laughing like a lunatic. "You boys are under the duckweed!" Lufroy shouts. "Very smart, but I'll find you now!" He's scanning the water intently as he makes his way back to the log to take a breather. The boys see that he's decided to sit on the log right where the snake had been and that his feet are now on the same side where the boys had been hiding. After a five-minute rest, he picks up the branch that he'd used earlier to shoo the snake away, and starts poking it into the duckweed as he retraces his search pattern.

Billy's eyes meet Nick's and he communicates a mental message: *If you hadn't got us out of there we'd be in serious trouble right now!*

Nick winks his agreement and motions his head towards a cypress tree about two feet away. Making his way slowly, he comes to rest in a hollow created by the unique trunk of the tree. Billy slides in next to him. They're now hidden in the shadows, which are starting to slowly reclaim the swamp as the sun, past its highest point, continues its journey to the west.

Several minutes pass as the boys watch Lufroy move farther away. "How you doing, man?" Nick whispers so quietly his words can barely be heard.

"I'm hungry and dying of thirst," Billy responds with a pained expression on his face. "All this water and we can't drink it. I won't be caring about the bacteria before long."

As Billy's talking, he can see that his friend is reaching with his arms towards his feet. Straightening, Nick comes up with a sock that he very slowly brings above the water's surface. He wrings out as much swamp water as he can. He then reaches toward the trunk of the tree and begins scraping the red, spongy fungus-like stuff from the bark, shoving several handfuls into his sock until the entire foot section is packed.

"This is red sphagnum moss," he whispers. "It holds ten times its weight in moister." He hands the sock over to Billy. "Squeeze the moss and let the water drip into your mouth."

Not only does this moss hold moister and work as a good filter, it also contains natural iodine which will disinfect the water.

Slowly, Billy takes the offered sock, and without a second thought, just as slowly moves it into position. As he squeezes the sock, a slow, steady stream of water begins falling into his mouth. The moss-filled sock produces about a mouth full of water, and it's great. His body needed this so badly that Billy's normal critiquing standards for food and beverage don't apply. When survival depends on something, the body desires *only* that, not caring about where it comes from or what it tastes like.

Meanwhile, Nick has removed his other sock and is filling it with moss for himself. Once he gets his small, but delicious drink, they empty the contents from the socks so he can put them and his boots back on. He needs to be ready in case they have to start running again.

The shadows are growing steadily and Lufroy's visibility and distance are working in their favor. "Okay, I think it's time we distance ourselves further," Nick whispers. "Let's try to keep moving until we can safely stand and find our way home."

The boys set off, moving out of the shadows of the cypress trees, to begin slowly making their way farther from this dangerous man.

CHAPTER 14

Missing

By 3:45 p.m., Nick's and Billy's moms had worked themselves into the tizzy that Nick had predicted. At 1:30, Nick's mom, Sue, had received a call from a concerned Annie, asking if the boys had returned from their camping trip and were by chance hanging out at her house. Once Sue informed her that they had *not* returned, their conversation only served to cause both moms to start panicking and visualizing the boys out there in the swamp...lost or hurt.

Annie finally told Sue that she would call Ben to tell him to come home and go out to the boys' campsite. When she got Ben on the phone he told her to calm down, the boys had probably lost track of time in their exploring. He informed her that if they hadn't made it home by the time he returned from work he would walk out there to get them.

"But Ben," Annie had responded, still terribly worried, "don't you think it's more than coincidence that Mr. Pierre was scared out of the swamp a few days ago and then the boys are late to return home today? I think I should call the sheriff and have him organize a search party."

This caused Ben to pause a moment. He had forgotten about Mr. Pierre. "Okay, baby, call the sheriff and let him know about Mr. Pierre and the boys being late. Tell him that I'll be home by four and plan to go get the boys. I'm sure he can't do anything right now with the boys being just a couple hours overdue, but it won't hurt to have him ready in case we need his help.

"I hope they show up soon, Ben," Annie said. "I'm really getting worried."

"Just stay calm, Annie. You know how the boys are when it comes to them getting together out there. Filling the sheriff in on what's going on is about all we can do now."

"I'll do just that right now. Okay, I'll see you soon. I just hope they're back by the time you get here." She'd hurriedly hung up the phone and rushed to the magnet on the refrigerator where all of the local emergency phone numbers were listed.

"Police Department," said a bored sounding voice on the other end of the line.

"I need to speak to Sheriff Leger right away." Annie's voice was far from bored sounding.

"May I ask who's calling?"

"This is Annie Boudreaux."

"Hi Annie, this is Kim. How have y'all been?"

"Listen Kim, I'm sorry, but I really gotta speak to the sheriff. Nick and Billy haven't made it back from their camping trip yet and I'm really worried."

"Oh my God, okay, hold on just a sec," Kim said as she placed Annie on hold.

"Sheriff Leger," a man's voice said after a short wait. Sheriff Lester Leger was nearly the same age as Annie. They'd been classmates right up until high school graduation when he'd gone on to graduate from the police academy to become a deputy. Five years later he was voted in as sheriff. He took great pride in his community and his position as its protector. Born and raised in Pierre Part, he knew every family within his district and would do whatever was necessary to see no harm ever came to any of them.

"Lester, its Annie Boudreaux. I'm calling because Billy and Nick went camping last night and haven't made it home yet."

"Hello there Annie, you know how those boys are. If they got busy on some project out there they've probably forgotten all about the time."

"I've already spoken to Ben and he'll go look for them when he gets home around four, if they haven't made it back yet. But he wanted me to call you to tell you something else that concerns us." Annie went on to explain everything she knew about Mr. Pierre being scared out of the swamp by what he thought was the Rougarou, and their feeling that they feared it wasn't just a coincidence that all of this has happened in the same week.

The sheriff listened to this intently and when she finished giving her version of the events that had occurred these past few days his concern started to grow. He wasn't a believer in coincidence, but hearing that a tough man like Pierre had been frightened away from his home by a monster, a few days before the boys are late returning home from the same swamp, caused a feeling of foreboding to settle in his gut.

"Annie, I want you to call me as soon as the boys make it home or when Ben has made it back from going out to get them at their camp. I'm going to make a few calls and start rounding up volunteers in case we need to send out a search party. I'm also going to get in touch with Pierre to hear his story again." Lester paused for an instant. "Don't worry, Annie, we'll have those boys back home as soon as we can. Don't forget to call me back like I asked, okay?"

"Okay, Lester. Thank you so much."

As soon as she'd hung up the phone she'd written Ben a short note telling him where she would be, then she'd bee-lined it over to Sue's house.

Now at four o'clock in the afternoon, she sits with her friend at the dining room table waiting for Ben to arrive. For the past two hours they'd sat silently, not wanting to miss the sound of laughter should the two boys make their way up the trail from the swamp and into the backyard. So far this wait has produced only heartache.

Without knocking, Ben marches through the front door. As he enters the kitchen, his wife is already on her feet throwing herself into his arms and releasing the flood of tears she's been holding back all afternoon.

"Now, now baby, we'll find the boys," he says. His voice is full of the emotions that have been building in him throughout the afternoon.

Still in her seat at the table, Sue begins to cry. "Please, Ben," she pleads softly, "get out there and find the boys. I just know something's wrong."

Stepping back from the embrace of his wife, Ben walks toward the back door. As he steps outside, he says over his shoulder, "I'll be back as soon as I can, girls."

Running down the trail, Ben is scared. If something's happened to either of the boys, he doesn't know how he'll be able to live with himself. It was because of his having brushed off his wife's fear for the boys camping out after Mr. Pierre's warning that they were out there in the first place. As the dirt turns to mud and the mud turns to water he doesn't slow down. A cottonmouth is laying on the trail in peaceful bliss one second and the next, it's flying through the air as Ben rushes through. The camp comes into view up ahead. He races up the steps and opens the door…nobody! Two sleeping bags, that appear to have not been slept in, are spread out on the floor. When Ben sees this, total panic sets in. He swings his head outside the door. "Billy! Nick! Can you hear me? Billy!"

He storms down the stairs and, thoughtless of the direction he's heading, instinctively rushes off to begin searching. Coming quickly to his senses, he stops. He needs to get to a phone to call the sheriff without delay. It'll be dark in three more hours and he needs as many eyes as possible out here searching.

He hits the trail back to civilization at full speed. The fear he feels at the thought of the boys being hurt causes profuse sweating and shortness of breath. He recalls nothing of his mad dash up the trail as he finds himself suddenly opening the back door to the Landry house and rushing into the kitchen. Sue and Annie immediately stand up and voice their questions, but Ben ignores them and rushes to the phone. Glancing at the refrigerator to read the number he wants from the list, he makes the call he's been dreading all afternoon that he might have to make.

"Get me Lester, this is Ben Boudreaux."

Crying softly, the boys' moms move together in an embrace.

"Lester, I just went out to the boys' camp and they aren't there. It doesn't look like they slept in their sleeping bags last night, either." Ben hears a moan start up from the women as the panic they've been trying to hold at bay turns to dread.

"Ben, I have two dozen volunteers waiting for my call," Sheriff Leger says firmly at the other end of the line. "Kim, Tim!" he shouts away from the phone, his voice slightly muffled. "Get on the phone and start calling those volunteers. Tell 'em we'll meet at Sid Landry's house as soon as possible!"

"I'll be there in five minutes, Ben," he says, returning to the conversation. "Just hang in there, buddy. We'll have all the men I was able to contact, out in that swamp looking for the boys in a half hour."

Without replying, Ben hangs up and turns to the women. "The boys are missing. I'm so sorry." He walks to a chair and sits down. The exhaustion from running and the shock from not being able to find the boys washes over his solid, muscular frame. He looks at Sue holding onto his wife. "I think you should contact Sid and have him call for a chopper to bring him in. Tell him the sheriff will be here in half an hour with two dozen men to start a search."

CHAPTER 15

Lost

It's been at least fifteen minutes since the boys last spotted Lufroy, who was still poking and prodding the water with the tree branch. His threats and off-the-wall ramblings are just barely audible as the shadows begin to seriously take control of the swamp once more.

"I think we've gotten away, buddy," Billy whispers as they continue their slow, backward elbow walk. "What say we stand up?"

Nick was thinking of saying those same words, but Billy beat him to it. "Yeah, I think we should. My skin is shriveled so bad my fingers are starting to split and I think I'm getting trench foot. Besides, it's gonna be dark soon, so we need to find a place where we can stay dry overnight."

They cautiously stand up, instinctively keeping their heads low to decrease the size of their profiles. The first thing they do is fashion new walking sticks from the branches of a not-so-long dead tree standing nearby. As Billy takes the lead, Nick tells him to keep an eye out for anything they might be able to eat. It's critical that they find food to give them the energy they'll need to continue their journey the following day.

By walking, they're able to put much greater distance between themselves and Lufroy. A feeling of relief sweeps through them, as they seem to have gotten past this first obstacle. For the next half hour, before Nick even considers looking for a place to rest for the night, they continue walking, trying their best to minimize the noise they make. He's thankful to still have the flashlight that Lufroy had given him the night before when he was forced to lead the group back to the criminals' campsite. But he doesn't want to use it to walk through the water tonight. It's imperative that they find a dry spot so their skin can dry completely before they continue on their way in the morning. Once they find a dry place they'll be able to rehydrate and nurse their wounds.

But…Nick's getting worried. In another half hour, the swamp will be completely swallowed up by darkness. He's somewhat relieved, though, when he spots a cluster of cattails. And a dream-come-true occurs when, just beyond, he spots a small island of dry land. It's a small section, about ten by twenty feet, but right now it's as valuable as the entire state of Texas. As they step onto the dry land, both boys collapse. They're dehydrated, malnourished, and thoroughly exhausted.

"I don't think I've ever been this worn out," Nick says.

"Ain't that the truth!"

"After we rest a minute why don't you go pull up a few of those cattails? I'll start putting us a shelter together."

Fifteen minutes later, while Billy is collecting potassium-rich cattails, Nick breaks branches off of a few nearby palmetto bushes and lays the fronds out to make dry bedding. He wishes he had some twine to fasten branches to a tree to elevate their bed off the ground, but time and lack of materials aren't in their favor. By the time Billy returns with a nice energy-boosting meal, Nick has finished laying out the bedding fronds. He walks over to some nearby logs and scrapes off a good bit of red sphagnum moss. After collecting a sufficient amount, which he brings back to their sleeping spot, he heads back out for something else that's caught his eye. He returns carrying a couple handfuls of a long-stemmed weed with small white flowers.

"What's that for?" Billy asks.

"It's alligator weed. I read someplace that the leaves are as good as some of the stuff you find in salads. We just can't eat more than a few ounces of it. Something to do with getting too much calcium ox-a…oxa something. I don't remember exactly, but it's supposed to be toxic if you eat too much."

Billy breaks a leaf off to sample its flavor. "It's not as good as a cheeseburger but it's just as good as anything green that you'd find in a salad. I'm so hungry now that I'll enjoy this very much. But, why did you bring so much if we can't eat a bunch of it?"

"I read that the Chinese use it as an antibacterial and antiviral medication," Nick informs his friend. "I thought we could smash it up and rub the juice on our cuts to help with infection. These rope burns on our wrists and those cuts on your face aren't looking too good. Crawling through this swamp water all day has only helped the infection set in, not to mention the jungle rot that's started on my feet."

"What are you, a freaking encyclopedia?"

"I'm not an encyclopedia. I just read things that might help me one day." Nick lays the weeds on their make-shift bed. "And aren't you glad I did?" he adds jokingly.

"Heck yeah, I am! If it was just me I would already be sick from eating a belly full of raw crawfish."

"I really wish we had matches," Nick says, thinking of how good a handful of peeled crawfish would be right about now. "We don't have a pot to boil them in but we could sure roast some up and I bet that's some good stuff. We could also roast some frog legs as a side!"

While resting, and filling their bellies on cattail stalks and alligator weed their usual enthusiastic spirit begins to take over again. They quietly laugh at each other's jokes and even begin joking about this being an adventure that they would be telling their grandkids about some day.

As the mosquitoes become more and more bothersome, the boys head out in search of branches and more palmetto fronds. They quickly put these together to form a small structure that's quite effective at keeping the tiny bloodsuckers at bay.

Inside the crudely built hut, in the red beam of the flashlight, they work at crushing the stems and leaves of the alligator weed and applying the juice generously to the wounds that cover their bodies from head to toe. Once this is done they stretch out and stare up at their makeshift ceiling and watch the small, black swamp ants walking on the underside of the palmetto fronds.

"Tomorrow morning we need to be up when the sun rises," Nick says following a few minutes of silent contemplation. "Seeing as how it rises in the east, we need to figure out the best direction we can travel to come out fairly close to Swamp Camp. I'm guessing that since we came out to Lost Bayou on a compass heading of fifty degrees, we'd need to reverse that direction to make it back. That's two hundred thirty degrees on the compass, which is nearly in a southwest heading."

"But what about the distance we traveled along the bayou and then the direction we took to get to where we are now? That'll definitely put us off track pretty bad," Billy replies after seeing the obvious dilemma this strategy presents.

"Yes, you're right. Let me think on it for a bit." Nick becomes quiet as he visualizes the map that they'd studied the day before. He can see in his mind the straight line of their route to Lost Bayou and then the left turn they'd taken. He continues and passes the location of Mr. Pierre's place, coming to a stopping point at his best guess as to where the criminals had been holed up. Now, assuming they'd gone in a straight line out from this location, and assuming they'd traveled the same distance as what it took to get from Swamp Camp to Lost Bayou, they should be right here, he tells himself as he places an imaginary finger at that spot on the virtual map. The line from this point back to Swamp Camp seems to be in a southeast heading.

Quickly breaking pieces off of the alligator weed, Nick begins reconstructing the map, as he pictures it in his head, laying out the pieces of weed on their leafy bedding so that Billy can visualize it. After he's laid out markers for Swamp Camp, Lost Bayou, Mr. Pierre's place, a best guess as to the location of the criminals' hide-out, and their present location, he goes on to explain the compass headings that he remembers and his best guesses as to what the new heading should be to bring them out of the swamp close to Swamp Camp's location.

Thoroughly impressed by his friend's ability to reconstruct—from memory—their travel route and go on to figure a way home from their present unknown location, Billy shakes his head in amazement. "Remind me that if I ever get lost again to make sure you're with me. It's totally nuts the way you figured that out in your head and made it look totally logical for me. You're like Spock!"

They both laugh at this comparison to the legendary *Star Trek* figure.

"Let's just hope this works and I don't end up getting us lost deeper in the swamp." A lot is riding on Nick's shoulders with his calculations. If they're still lost by the next sunset, he knows that the infection that's beginning to set in will create a life-and-death struggle for them. Once they become too weak to continue moving, there won't be much hope of them ever being found.

"I have faith in you, Nick. I think we better get some rest so we don't miss the sun coming up. I feel so tired that I might end up sleeping until tomorrow afternoon."

"Yeah, let's get some sleep. We can't afford to oversleep in the morning." Nick stretches out on the bedding and rolls onto his side. As he closes his eyes his thoughts are of his family and how frantic they must be right now.

CHAPTER 16

The Search

Sheriff Leger looks around the table at the despondent faces of those sitting around him. As the hours have slipped by since the two-man search teams entered the swamp, his three friends have slipped deeper and deeper into themselves. When he'd arrived here, they were full of frantic energy, all wanting to talk to him at once and moving around in uncertain directions. That was preferable to the silence and vacant stares he was witnessing now. He can't help but place himself in their situation. His son, Sonny, is about the same age as their boys, and he knows that he'd be devastated if it was Sonny who was lost out there in that dark swamp.

He looks at the wall clock and sees that it's eleven o'clock. He then looks down at the display screen on his laptop, which is showing a detailed map of the swamp. Each team is carrying a GPS receiver that not only allows them to always know their location but also transmits that location to the sheriff's computer. Thirteen tiny red dots appear on the screen, representing each team's present location, and a light blue trail marks the route each red dot has taken. This lets him see where each team has searched, allowing him to increase his ability to be as efficient in the search as possible. He's happy with the way they all appear evenly fanned out from the location of the boy's camp, but not with the painfully slow pace the night has caused.

All of these volunteers have grown up in this area and know that nighttime in the swamp must be respected. The things that can cause harm to a person are hidden in the shadows, so it's wise to slow down and be certain that it's safe to take the next step or that no potential hazards exist on any tree or stump where you might place your hand.

Suddenly, an excited voice booms out from the radio's speaker. "Come in, Sheriff, Team-7 here." All vacant stares instantly transform into looks conveying hope.

The sheriff picks up his radio. "Sheriff, here."

"Sheriff, this is Luke. Lewis has been bit by a gator."

The sheriff looks down at his laptop screen and sees that Team-7 is located on the west side of the search area. "How's he doing, Luke? Do you need a medic sent your way?"

"No, Sir. He says he can walk fine, so we'll go ahead and head in now. It was about a six-footer that lunged out of the water and grabbed his hand. With both of us wrestling it, the darn thing still wouldn't turn loose and I had to shoot it. Lewis'll need some stitches and should be checked for any problems we can't see. "

"Roger that, Luke. You two head back to Sid's and I'll let the paramedics outside know that you're on the way." Sheriff Leger looks down at the table thoughtfully for a moment. "Sheriff, to all teams," he says into the radio. "I'll be calling off the search at midnight and resuming at six in the morning. It's now eleven ten. If any of you feel like heading back in now, go ahead. I don't expect you to remain out there at night."

The parents of the missing boys look at the sheriff. They want the search to continue but they understand the danger their neighbors are putting themselves in. They get up from their seats and, together, the three of them come to stand silently behind the sheriff for a peek at the laptop screen. As they watch, all of the red dots continue moving away from the starting point. There's not a dry eye in the room, and they can feel the intense love and protection their community offers. Pierre Part is a small, extremely close, almost clannish community. The different families have lived together for so many generations that they've formed one big family that's furiously protective of each and every member.

People from large cities will never enjoy the phenomena of community solidarity as small towns do. City people can often be quick to judge, referring to small town people as hicks and thinking they're ignorant and lazy but, truth be told, those that grow up in the country are typically raised with strong family values that stress the importance of education, faith, hard work, and offering a helping hand to those in need. Perhaps the biggest benefit of living in the country is that the children are far removed from the influence of gangs and drug lords. Many country folk feel pity for the families raising their children in the city, where there are so many negative influences and where it's often difficult for vulnerable kids to focus on the positive lessons their parents try to teach them.

The sheriff steps outside to inform the paramedics that a man suffering from a gator bite will be coming in soon. He then returns to join the group waiting in the kitchen. "I'll need these men to come in and get some rest tonight. They need to be sharp when we start again in the morning."

"I agree," Ben says hesitantly. "I'm certain those boys have found shelter for the night. And we don't need anyone else to get hurt…or worse. Sid'll be back by then. And Lester, I want you to give us one of those GPS trackers so we can join in on the search. I can't sit here anymore while the boys are gone."

"You got it, Ben. I'm sorry to have kept you from going tonight, but you were in no shape to stay focused. I hope you can understand that," the sheriff explains to his friend once again. He'd barely been able to hold Ben back when the search parties had left the house earlier but he knew he had no choice. Ben was beside himself with worry and wouldn't have done any good out there.

"If I didn't understand your reasoning, Lester, there would've been no way you could've held me back. I've had time to let it settle in and I'll be able to help tomorrow. And I'm sure Sid will be level-headed enough to team up with me by morning." Ben looks over at his wife and Sue. "I give you my word that we *will* find them tomorrow."

The ladies can only nod their heads in response. They've been silent all evening, still overcome with shock and worry.

"Ladies, do you think you can get a couple of cold waters ready for Luke and Lewis when they get back here?" the sheriff asks in an attempt to help them overcome their shock. "I'm sure they could really use a cold drink."

That seemed to be exactly what was needed. "Yes, of course," the ladies respond in unison and together set about filling glasses with ice and water. They even prepare a glass for each person in the house and bring a couple more out to the paramedics waiting in the ambulance parked in the driveway.

Shortly after the ladies return to the kitchen, Sid comes crashing through the door. His fear has been held in check since his wife called to pass on Ben's message, and as the hours slipped by while he waited on the chopper and during the long, five-hour drive from

Galveston, his anxiety had built to an almost painful level. By the time he made it home, shouldering his way into his house, he was in the midst of mental chaos. He's had no one to talk to all day and his active imagination has invented dozens of different scenarios for what has happened to the boys.

Unable to speak and needing to feel the touch of a loved one, Sid rushes to his wife for an embrace. Several minutes pass as his friends offer him consoling words. He turns to the sheriff, asking to be brought up to speed on the search, and sits there silently, and thoughtfully, as the sheriff gives him the details.

Just as the sheriff is finishing his update, Luke knocks on the back door, announcing his and Lewis' arrival. Annie jumps up to greet them. "I'm so sorry, Lewis! Are you okay?" she asks, handing them each a glass of water, which they gratefully accept.

"What, this?" Smiling, Lewis holds up his bandaged hand. "Please, Annie, my wife's cat has caused me more serious injuries."

It's obvious from the red wetness that has soaked through the dressing that it isn't as simple as a cat scratch. A tearful Annie gives Lewis a hug, thanking him for his help.

The sheriff escorts Lewis to the ambulance and instructs Luke to go on home for some rest and to be back here at 6:00 a.m. sharp. He returns to the kitchen and picks up his radio. "Sheriff, to all teams, the search is now being suspended until six tomorrow morning. Go ahead and make your way back now."

After all of the teams have acknowledged the sheriff's instructions, he turns to the parents of the missing boys. "Please, try to get some rest. We'll all need to be sharp tomorrow and not miss any hints pointing to where the boys might have gone."

"You're right, Lester," Ben nods in agreement. "We'll be back here at five-thirty tomorrow morning. What about you two?" he asks looking at Sid and Sue. "Will you be up?"

"Yes, we'll be up," Sue answers. "Y'all come by and we can get some coffee and biscuits ready for when the men show up."

Ben and Annie give their friends a hug and make their way home for an attempt at getting some sleep, though they know it'll be a restless night.

"I'll go on out and meet the men coming in from the swamp," the sheriff says to Sid and Sue. "You two try to get some rest and I'll see you in the morning."

Saying their goodnights, the Landry's shut the door with hopes that this nightmare will end tomorrow.

Lufroy looks at his watch—*12:35 a.m.* That means he's been searching this area repeatedly for about twelve hours now. He's exhausted and knows it. It's time to give up and get his boat taken care of.

With a curse he flings his stick away and hollers out to the boys that are sleeping soundly out of earshot. "You little twerps are so freaking lucky I didn't find you! Hope to see you again someday!" And with that he starts back to his camp. Luckily, the light from the moon is still bright enough for him to see his way since his flashlight battery had died hours earlier. Even still, it's a slow trip because of the obstacles hidden in shadow.

After an hour of trudging through the swamp, he finally makes it back to his shack. He's so worn out that sleep is all that he can think of. Bailing out the boat will have to wait for morning.

He glances over at his cousin in disgust. Gator Bait's head looks like a watermelon it's swollen so badly, and it doesn't appear that he's moved an inch since Lufroy landed his last kick just before noticing that the boys were gone and he was forced to give chase.

Lufroy moves over to stand beside his cousin lying prone on the ground, and noticing that his chest is neither rising nor falling, gives him a final kick. He turns away from Gator Bait's body and stumbles into the shack where he falls onto the pile of blankets on the floor, instantly asleep.

CHAPTER 17

Snake Bit

At five thirty the next morning, Ben and Annie enter the Landry home. All four friends are mentally drained but eager to get this day underway. They gather in the kitchen and the women immediately begin filling thermoses with coffee and cutting biscuits to bake for the men who'll be arriving shortly.

Sheriff Leger arrives and sets up his command post on the table as he did the day before. He tests all of the GPS units to make certain he's able to receive the data they each provide. He hands one of the units to Ben, who's sitting next to him. "This is for you and Sid. You'll replace Luke and Lewis as Team-7. I've entered new waypoints in all of these units so we don't have to search the exact same path the men took last night."

"Good idea, Lester," Ben says. "With a good fourteen hours of daylight we'll be able to cover a lot of ground today."

Sharing his thoughts, Sid joins the conversation. "I just don't see how we can't *not* find them today with this many people searching. They didn't just disappear. If we don't find them today then there's a good chance that we never will. We *have got* to find them today!"

"Let's not go there until we need to," the sheriff says. "Let me remind you that this is still a search and rescue operation, not a recovery operation. Don't let your thinking go in that direction, okay, guys?" After he receives a nod from each of them, he determines that he'd best help his friends to stay positive and in the present. "I see the daylight starting, why don't you two head on out?"

Sid and Ben get up from the table and give their wives a hug before stepping outside; each saying a silent prayer that the boys are by their sides when they return.

As the search parties begin to trickle in, they're given GPS receivers and instructions, and immediately head off down the trail. By six o'clock, every member of the search party has already passed Swamp Camp, actively searching for the boys. The echoing shouts of the boys' names can be heard coming from any given direction.

As dawn begins to lighten the eastern sky, Nick opens his eyes. He's lying on his back, looking up to see the same tiny black swamp ants walking aimlessly on the bottom of the palmetto-frond ceiling. He hears his friend snoring lightly in his sleep. The past two days have been exhausting for both of them. Because of this, he's hesitant to wake Billy. Instead, he takes a moment to enjoy some of the things that have always soothed his spirit. He smells the rich and musky odor of the gases emitted by decaying vegetation and rising out of the water. He hears the birds that are already out searching for the juicy morsels that waited too long to retreat into their rotting homes. He hears the squirrels as they play an early morning game of chase through the treetops. He feels the dampness of the morning dew that coats his face and arms.

Inadvertently, his thoughts slowly make their way to his present predicament. It appears that they've made good their escape from Lufroy. Now his friend will be counting on him to get them home. He hasn't moved a muscle but can still feel that his body is weak. Combine that with the lightheadedness he's feeling and, that if his calculations were off, they're in serious trouble. Another day spent out here without being found and their situation will be dire. He's sure that by now there are people searching for them, so if he was close to calculating the correct direction for them to travel, they should eventually bump into someone. And if he was wrong and they traveled away from civilization then they'd probably never make it out alive.

He decides to put these dark thoughts out of his mind and think of a way that he might be able to cheer up his friend when he wakes up. He decides to cross his fingers and hope that the daylight will reveal some nice sweet blackberries growing somewhere in the area. It's doubtful, though, that he'll find any since they prefer damp soil—not twelve inch deep swamp water. But, hey, he'd found an island out in the middle of the swamp, so anything's possible.

He closes his eyes and says a silent prayer to the Man above that He help guide them down the path to home. As he says the prayer, he feels guilty that he's tried, every Sunday for as long as he can remember, to skip church. Especially during the school year, when only two days a week are available for exploring. Of course, he hadn't ever had a good enough excuse and the only time he'd ever been allowed to actually skip church was when he had chickenpox. And, in all honesty, he would much rather go to church than suffer all the discomfort associated with that ailment.

He opens his eyes and notices a bit of moisture seeping from behind his eyelids. He quickly wipes it away and moves to straighten his legs so that he can slide feet first out of the shelter. Instantly, he feels a weight slap against the inside of his ankle, followed by a burning pain that shoots up his leg like a lightning bolt. He quickly lifts his head and spots a water moccasin resting between his feet.

Sometime during the night, apparently, the snake had been out hunting and stumbled upon this nice, dry place in which to hide and wait in ambush for an unsuspecting mouse or frog. When it felt the force of Nick's leg push against it, the snake had struck instinctively. If Nick's jeans had been pulled down to cover his ankles, the fangs might have been deflected or not gone so deep, but they were riding high, mid-calf. The snake's sharp fangs went right through the fabric of his socks, unimpeded, to sink three-quarters of an inch into the muscle just inside his ankle.

Not knowing how far away Lufroy is, Nick doesn't want to make any sound at all, but this hurts so bad that it's impossible to hold back everything, and his muffled screams jolt Billy awake.

Billy's eyes follow the direction of his friend's gaze. He spots the snake, coiled up and ready to strike again. Without thought or hesitation, Billy grabs the stick lying beside him and gives the snake a sharp, powerful wallop over the head, killing it instantly. He quickly pushes it outside knowing that even a dead snake can still manage to bite. "Did it get you?" he shouts, but Nick can't answer because of the panic and pain. Billy flings himself toward his friend's feet and he notices blood soaking through Nick's sock. He pulls the sock down and what he sees causes him to pale—two visible fang marks. Blood is slowly seeping out of the punctures and the skin around the wound seems to be swelling and turning an angry reddish-orange color right before his eyes. "Oh my, God," he whispers.

Recalling what he'd been taught about snakebites, the first thing to do is keep the victim calm and as motionless as possible. He focuses his attention on trying to calm his friend. "Nick, you've been bitten," he says softly. "You gotta calm down to keep the poison from spreading."

His friend's quiet words seem to help. Nick stops sobbing and his eyes come back into focus. He looks at Billy. "What am I gonna do?" he asks in a low voice. "I need some help, but we don't even know where we are."

"We have no choice, Nick. I need to carry you out of here. I know you should lay still but there's no guaranty that I can find my way back here if I leave you. At least it bit you on the ankle, so I can carry you over my shoulder and the wound will stay below the level of your heart, which will slow down the spread of the venom."

"Are you sure you can carry me?" Concern shows clearly on Nick's face. "We don't know how far we gotta go and you're probably still worn out from yesterday, not to mention you're probably getting sick."

"I'll get you out of here, buddy. Don't you worry about that," Billy says with a confidence he hopes he can live up to.

"Just remember to keep the sun to your left side but slightly in front," Nick says quickly, recalling the route he'd plotted on his mental map. "Let's just hope I figured it right."

"Of course you figured it right," Billy says, trying to lighten the situation. "You're the Brainiac."

Nick grimaces in pain. "I think we need to start moving. I'm getting a headache and it's getting harder for me to breathe."

Knowing that these are some of the first symptoms to appear following a snake bite, Billy wastes no time. He stands straight up, throwing the roof of their shelter aside. Bending down next to his friend, he puts on his boots, and then helps Nick put his boot on his uninjured leg. Since Nick is able to stand upright, Billy easily brings him up and over his shoulder. Looking to where the rising sun is lighting the sky most brightly, Billy turns so that it's positioned slightly in front and to their left, and heads off at a brisk but safe pace.

Billy's concern for Nick is growing. They've been traveling for only about ten minutes, when he notices Nick struggling to breathe, and feels the heat coming from his body—a definite sign that fever is setting in. Billy's never been this afraid, but it's his fear that's distracting him from the aching muscles in his back, legs, and arms, and keeping him focused on his mission. He's determined to bring his friend to safety and that's the only thing he's living for at that moment.

CHAPTER 18

Footprints Spotted

Sean and Steve, members of Team-3, have been assigned a search area to the northeast of the boys' camp and they'd unknowingly been moving parallel to the trail the boys had cut to Lost Bayou. Once they'd reached the waterway, they'd turned north to follow the trail. It's now just before nine in the morning and they're walking along the high ground, their focus on finding anything that might not belong—evidence of the boys' passage.

"Look here, Sean," Steve says as he nods his head in the direction of a small patch of mud beside his left foot. "It looks like the front half of a boy's boot print."

Sean, looking down, agrees that the boot that made this impression is obviously small enough to have been made by a boy. Immediately, he pulls out his radio. "Sheriff, Team-3 here."

Back at his makeshift command post in the Landry's kitchen, Sheriff Leger responds to the incoming transmission. "This is the sheriff. Go ahead, Team-3."

"We found part of a boot print that might belong to one of the boys. It's small enough anyway."

Annie and Sue are on their feet instantly, coming around the table to get a look at the tracking map to see where Team-3 is located.

"Which direction does the print appear to be heading?" the sheriff asks as he pinpoints the team's location on the map.

"It's definitely heading north along the bayou...standby a sec."

"Standing by."

Ben's voice crackles over the radio. "What's Team-3's current location, Lester?"

"They're at Lost Bayou," the sheriff replies. "Just south of Mr. Pierre's place."

"That's where they headed, Lester!" Ben shouts, fear and panic evident in his voice. "They went out to see about whatever it was that scared off Mr. Pierre."

"Hold on a second, Ben, let's see why Team-3 told us to standby."

"Sheriff, Team-3 here, we found a wide patch of mud that shows clearly four sets of prints, two small sets that could be the boys and two larger sets. What's peculiar is that these prints seem to be walking on top of the same four sets that we noticed first, heading south." The radio is silent as Sean pauses for a second. "Sheriff, it looks like the boys might have been running away and maybe they were caught and being led back in this direction."

Before the sheriff can respond, Ben's voice comes loudly through the radio. "We gotta get out there, Lester! The boys could be in trouble!"

"Hold on a minute, Ben, let's think this through first," the sheriff responds, pausing while he mentally runs through the various options. Choosing half of the teams nearest to Team-3, he directs them to meet with Team-3 at their current location along Lost Bayou and to stand-by until he arrives. Once he's relayed the coordinates, he instructs the remaining teams to continue searching their assigned areas.

"Ben, I want you and Sid to head back here. You're too far west and it would be quicker if you come here, then we can take a boat out to Lost Bayou."

"We're on our way, Lester," Ben replies, his breathing coming hard through the radio.

While the sheriff waits for Ben and Sid to arrive, he gathers his computer and the radio link equipment he'll need in order to continue tracking the search party.

"What do you think this is all about, Lester?" Sue asks. "Do you think the boys are in trouble?"

"I just don't know, Sue. I'm concerned about those larger tracks Sean found, but let's not read too much into this just yet."

"The sheriff's right," adds Annie, refusing to accept the possibility that the boys are hurt or in serious trouble. "Maybe they're in the boat with the men right now and headed back!"

To keep the boys' moms from becoming even more upset, the sheriff agrees with her, but unlike them, he can't shake the feeling in his gut.   If Team-3 interpreted those prints correctly, someone's chasing those boys.

An hour later, breathless and soaking wet from their mad dash through the swamp, Ben and Sid rush into the house. They quickly assist the sheriff in carrying his equipment out to his car. On the way, the sheriff instructs the paramedics outside to remain where they are in case their assistance is needed on this end of the search operation.   He also asks them to radio dispatch to have another ambulance meet him at the boat slip with an emergency team prepared to travel with him in the boat.

They tear down the drive in the sheriff's car, burning rubber as they turn northeast onto the parish highway.

As they speed down the highway, cypress trees whizzing past on either side, Sid's thoughts are racing. "Lester," he says to the sheriff as he thinks of something that might help with their approach to Lost Bayou. "I was thinking about what Sean said about those tracks. Based on where they're located, it sounds like they're heading north along the bayou. Have you considered bringing the boat through Knobs Cut so we can come in from the south? We don't want to pass by the boys, and whoever those bigger tracks belong to, before we know they mean our boys no harm."

"That's an excellent idea, Sid. It's been years since I thought about that cut. It's shallow and mostly only good to go frogging on, but I think we'll have no problems getting my boat through."

They arrive at the marina parking lot and rush to load the boat with the gear they've brought with them. From the trunk of the car, the sheriff removes an assault rifle and shotgun, which he stows under a seat at the bow of his boat. As he cranks the engines to warm them up, the ambulance pulls into the lot and two emergency personnel jump out, carrying with them field kits full of medical supplies. As the paramedics climb aboard, the last rope is cast off and the boat begins backing out of the slip. All onboard are quiet as the sheriff steers the boat in the direction of Knobs Cut, and gives it full throttle.

As they speed along, dodging the debris that floats constantly on the bayou, Sid can't help but marvel at the beauty that surrounds his community. The clear, dark bayou waters that are like highways branching off in all directions provide countless creatures an abundance of food and sanctuary. *Please, God, let this land provide sanctuary to our boys.* He watches as the majestic bald cypress trees pass by, loaded with so much Spanish moss that it would seem to be a burden. And, now that he thinks about it, he realizes that's likely to be the case much of the time. While it's not a parasite that feeds off of the tree, the moss is very heavy and can cause some branches to break under its weight, and at times, large amounts of the moss can cover the leaves, affecting the tree's normal growth.

After ten minutes at full throttle the sheriff pulls back, causing the vessel to settle deeper into the water. "Ben, why don't you keep an eye off the bow to make sure I don't damage the prop on any stumps I can't see from this angle."

Ben takes his position on the bow as the sheriff swings the boat to track through the middle of Knobs Cut. As they putter along, a couple of four-foot-tall Great Blue Herons take flight. The sounds they make are totally different from what would be expected from such a beautiful creature. If you take the sound of a goose's honk and lengthen it to last about five seconds, then you'd be close to hearing what the men hear as they disturb the nice quiet place where the birds hunt for frogs, snakes, and fish. Off to the side along the shoreline, several large alligators create a loud splash as they make a quick departure from the logs they've been sunning on, and take refuge in the hidden world beneath the surface.

Ben suddenly points in front of the port bow. Spoken commands are not needed with this method of navigating hazardous waters. Ben keeps his finger pointed at the tip of a tree he sees lying below the water's surface to the left of the boat, allowing the sheriff to know exactly when he can bring the boat back into the center of the cut. After five minutes and no additional obstacles, the boat comes out onto Lost Bayou.

The sheriff turns right, on a north heading, and brings the motor to half throttle. They know the search party has gathered at the spot somewhere south of Mr. Pierre's, where they found the footprints, but they're not sure of the exact location. They keep their eyes peeled port side, and eventually see the twelve men on shore, flagging them down. The sheriff brings the vessel around and toward the bank, sliding the bow a foot's length along the muddy bank before coming to a stop. Ben, the first to jump from the boat, secures a line to a nearby tree. Once the gear has been offloaded, the men gather on the trail.

Team-3 shows the latest arrivals the tracks they've found and the men gather around the sheriff to listen to what he has to say. Sheriff Leger clears his throat and looks somberly at the men around him, each of them carrying a holstered sidearm for protection against any dangers that can't be avoided through simple measures. "I read those tracks just like y'all did, and if these bigger tracks belong to a couple bad guys then we might need every gun we have. And even though you're all armed, I didn't think it would be smart to have any of you running off and finding trouble on your own."

"We understand that, Sheriff," says Cecil Prejean, an old badger of a man who's not known for his patience on a good day, let alone in a situation like this. He's also Godfather to Billy's mom and extremely eager to get on with the search. "Now that everyone's here, what do you want to do?"

"Follow me and take it slow. Keep your eyes peeled for trouble or signs of the boys and stay to the edge of the trail so as not to ruin any of the tracks that are there. And, turn off all radios."

As the men power down their radios, the sheriff plugs in his radio headset so he can monitor any messages from the teams still out searching and not give warning to whoever's out there with the boys. Once he has the headset comfortably in place, the sheriff turns and slowly begins his trek north along the edge of the bayou.

CHAPTER 19

Struggles

Billy is breathing hard and ready to fall down to rest for the remainder of the day. Only the sounds of his friend's labored breathing keep him going. The last few times, when he'd asked Nick how he was doing, his friend hadn't answered, and now Billy's panicking. Nick must be unconscious and if Billy doesn't dig deep within himself and get him to safety, he's probably going to die.

He stops for a second to check his friend's wound. Lifting the leg of Nick's jeans he sees that the snakebite has swollen so much it's the size of a lemon. The red area around the wound is actually starting to turn black as the venom kills the flesh. Billy knows that the toxic venom will rapidly destroy all the tissue it comes in contact with as it works its way outward.

As the day progressed and the sun has risen higher, the simple navigational instructions that he'd been given are becoming very difficult. It seems to be more of a guessing game now. Once the sun was no longer to his left but overhead, he'd begun eyeballing the farthest tree he could see, and once arriving at that tree, he'd eyeball the next tree in what he hoped to be the same direction. After using this method for the past hour he could only pray that he was still going in the desired direction and not just making wide circles. If this is what's happening, then Nick's as good as dead.

Billy's drawing deeper within himself than he's ever had to for energy and focus when his friend's body suddenly stiffens, then starts to convulse.

Sobbing, he drops down to one knee and swings Nick off his shoulder. Being careful to keep his friend's face out of the water, Billy cradles his convulsing body in his arms. He wants so very badly to do something more for his friend besides holding him still so he won't harm himself, but there's nothing else he can do—and it's killing him.

After the longest two minutes of Billy's life, Nick's seizure passes. He doesn't look good and his breathing is so labored that it seems it might stop at any moment.

Billy's sobbing heavily now. "Come on, buddy. You gotta make it! You ain't ever quit at nothing so don't do it now. I ain't quitting, either!" A new surge of energy courses through him, and he decides to carry his friend in his arms to make him more comfortable. This slows him down a bit but he's hoping the extra comfort might lessen the shock on his friend's body.

As his legs continue slicing through the water, he continuously glances down at Nick. The sweat seems to be coming off him at a steady stream and his wound is bleeding heavily from the venom, which is causing his blood to stop clotting.

Happy memories flit through Billy's mind as the thought of losing his friend becomes more and more of a possibility. Just about every day of his life has been shared with Nick and the adventures they've shared are epic. He remembers the night they'd been fishing for catfish with trout lines and he'd fallen from the boat when they hit a log. Nick had saved him from a large alligator that had been following them, waiting for pieces of fish or bait to be discarded, as they traveled from one line to the next. Of course they'd laughed about it once Nick had hoisted Billy back into the boat by his life vest. He thinks of the many times their families have gotten together for weekend crawfish boils, cook outs, and camping trips. Lots of laughs and stories had been shared on those days. He recalls how Nick is the only person in the world that he can share *everything* with. He can talk about girls or things that are bothering him and he never has to fear others ever finding out about them. He doesn't know how he can ever have fun in life again if his friend doesn't make it.

Billy reaches the tree he's been moving towards and focuses his attention on another one on the other side of it. He's about five steps into this latest march from point A to point B when he trips on a branch hidden from view by his friend's body. As he falls, he's expecting—just like several times earlier today—for his knees to sink into the mud below the surface. He's *not* expecting the lightning bolt of pain that shoots up his leg when his knee comes down squarely on a cypress stump sticking up about five inches from the muddy bottom.

His scream pierces the swamp, silencing the chatter of all the birds, insects, and reptiles. Yet, even in excruciating pain he never allows Nick's head to become submerged in the water. He sits down on the muddy bottom and straightens out his injured leg. The pain is so bad that he nearly blacks out. The sweat suddenly pours from him as he fights against the dizziness threatening to cause him to let go of his friend's head. While moaning from the pain, he focuses intently on not letting go until he's certain that the dizziness has passed and he won't let his friend down.

He sits motionless for several long minutes so he can gather himself once again. Then, slowly, he draws his foot in to bring his knee above the water's surface. After carefully pulling up the cuff of his jeans, he spots two leaches attached to his calf but ignores them as he continues uncovering his leg. When his knee is visible he sees that the skin has been peeled back over his kneecap. Gently he explores his knee with his fingertips to feel for any obvious broken bones. He breathes a sigh of relief as his kneecap seems to still be where it should be and in one piece.

He makes an attempt to stand, but when he tries to bend his knee to get it under him, the pain is too excruciating and he instantly sits back down. He's in a real bind…and his friend is counting on him!

With a look of determination on his face, Billy uses his hands to keep his friend lying in the same position in the water, and lifts himself into a standing position on his good leg. He tests his bad leg and can feel that his knee wants to give out. *I can't give up!* Distributing his weight evenly on both legs, he's hit by a feeling of nausea. He remains motionless in this position until his stomach settles, then slowly lifts Nick out of the water and into a carrying position, cradled against his chest. *I can do this!*

Billy sets out once again, limping heavily, determination alone driving him forward to the next tree in his sights.

CHAPTER 20

Bad Guys

The eighteen-man search team, plus two paramedics, makes its way north along Lost Bayou, occasionally spotting the four separate tracks, assuring them that they're still on the right path. As they come onto Mr. Pierre's land, they see that the tracks lead to the house. The men immediately slow down, become quiet, and train their weapons on the house. As they draw nearer, however, the tracks continue across the yard and turn back toward the bayou, ultimately continuing north along its bank.

Ben and Sid can hardly control their urge to rush forward. Only because the boys' lives might depend on stealth, are they able to hold this urge at bay and follow the sheriff's lead. The emotions they're experiencing are so jumbled that they're literally torturing themselves. Their thoughts are centered on them holding their sons very soon. But what shape will they be in when they're held? The different possibilities that come to mind create a very wide range of feelings.

The sheriff comes to a sudden stop, and Ben, so distracted by the insane number of chaotic thoughts in his head, walks straight into his back. He can only nod his head in response when the sheriff turns and casts a set of inquisitive eyes upon him.

Turning his attention back to the ground in front of him, the sheriff points out the rotting log that has a clear depression in the bark made by a small foot passing through it. He speaks quietly to the men gathering in close. "Those are handprints in the mud around this log. From the looks of it, I'd say one of the boys got his foot caught in it and was trying to get out in a hurry. We're definitely on the right trail."

He continues, cautiously, to lead his men, occasionally stopping to listen for sounds that might reveal any dangers up ahead. It's at the third such stop past the rotting log, that he hears something. He holds up his hand to warn the men following behind him, and then turns to look at them, holding a finger to his lips. As they listen intently, they can hear what sounds like someone grunting.

The sheriff crouches down low and continues moving at a very slow pace. As he comes around a small curve in the trail, he sees a huge man, one knee in the mud, pushing off with the other foot as he tries to pull a submerged aluminum boat up onto the bank.

The lower portion of the man's face is shielded from view by his shoulder as he struggles to slowly bring the vessel ashore. Seconds later he lifts his head to take in a deep breath of air and the sheriff instantly recognizes him.

The tensing of the sheriff's body does not go unnoticed by the men behind him. Moving seemingly as one, they unfasten their holsters and withdraw their weapons.

The sheriff turns around, dropping down to one knee, and the men huddle in closely around him. "That's Lufroy Aucoin over there by the boat," he whispers, "the escaped convict from Angola. The boys are definitely in trouble if he's found them. Right now his attention is on that boat. Let's quietly make our way into the clearing. I'm going to go straight for that shelter in case the boys are in there with whoever it was that made that second set of large footprints. You men keep an eye on Lufroy. Don't shoot him unless he leaves no other option."

The men move silently into the clearing. They're all experienced hunters who learned long ago how and where to place their feet for maximum silence in this wet and dangerous world. The dirty, grunting giant of a man struggling beside his boat never suspects a thing, until he hears the sound of the shack door being shattered and the shout of "Sheriff! Freeze!" as the sheriff fearlessly follows the barrel of his pistol into the dark interior of the shack.

Lufroy whips his head around to see what's causing this ruckus and spots a group of men standing nearby, their weapons pointing at him. As he listens to someone rummaging around inside his shack, two of the men in the group throw their weapons to the ground and, with a look of murder in their eyes, charge at him. Just before they make contact, a few of the others in the group quickly grab hold of them preventing them from doing whatever it is they plan to do to him.

"Haahaaahaaaaa!" The laughter suddenly and surprisingly erupts from Lufroy's belly. He just can't control it. After everything he's been through and all his careful planning, two *kids* are his down fall.

The sheriff exits the shack. "Lufroy, put your hands on your head and get down on your knees!"

Lufroy lowers his weary body to rest on his knees and the sheriff, removing a set of handcuffs from the case on his belt, secures Lufroy's wrists behind his back. Grabbing him by the wrists, the sheriff roughly brings him to his feet.

Lufroy is spun around to face the sheriff and the men standing behind him. "Where're your partner and the boys?" the sheriff asks.

So, the boys never did make it home. This must be the search party looking for them.

"Well, Sheriff, my partner is Gator Bait, and the last I seen him, he was laying there in that spot," Lufroy says, indicating with a nod of his head, a spot off to the side. "And judging by those gator tracks and the mud leading from the bayou to that spot, I'd say he got drug off during the night...as supper. He might'a been one ignorant excuse for a man but it appears he certainly lived up to his name."

"Where're my son and his friend?" Ben shouts out while making another effort to get at Lufroy's throat.

As the men around him once again hold Ben back, Lufroy laughs and looks over at Sid. "I'm guessing you're the other one's daddy, right? Well, let me be the first to admit that those two boys of yours are as sly and crafty as any man I've ever come up against. Not only did they get away but they put a hurtin' on me and my cousin. I'm surprised that gator would even consider Gator Bait as a meal," he says with a laugh, "considering the way he was looking after your boys got through with him."

The sound of Lufroy's laugher fills Sid and Ben with a feeling of dread. They don't trust this man who's capable of laughing as he talks about his own cousin's demise. But they realize that this monster might be the only key they have in finding their sons.

"Answer his question, Lufroy!" the sheriff demands. "When and where did you last see the boys?"

"Not here, but I can show you where they gave me the slip."

"Okay, lead the way and don't be foolish enough to try anything with all these men behind you. I have a feeling that I won't be able to control their trigger fingers if you make a break for it."

Lufroy doesn't want to return to prison, but he wants to be shot out here in the swamp even less. He quietly leads them out in the direction the boys had last traveled. Once he passes the tangle of vines that they'd disappeared behind, he sits on the same log he sat on the day before.

Lufroy gestures deeper into the swamp with a jerk of his chin, indicating to the men that this is where he last saw the boys. "I spent half the night searching for them and I'm certain they ducked down in this here duckweed and made their escape. You can see where I broke a branch off here to start prodding the water while I looked for them."

No one doubts that he's telling the truth. They know that Nick and Billy are smart enough to use their environment as a tool for escape and it's obvious that the branch Lufroy's pointing to has been broken off very recently.

The sheriff slips off his backpack and pulls out his laptop. He rests it on the log and powers it up. The map of the swamp appears, followed a second later by the red dots of the search parties. Half are still out there searching and the other half are clustered around the same log where the laptop is perched. He has to believe the boys are able to figure out a way to use the sun to navigate in a rough direction home. He directs the search parties that are out there to head for his current coordinates. He then turns to each team standing ready behind him and gives them a destination to head for from this point. The men fan out in the general direction of where the boys' camp is located.

The sheriff looks over at the two distraught fathers. "Would you two mind staying behind to help me watch this prisoner? We can head back to his hide-out and set up camp there, and I'd appreciate it if one you would get my boat and bring it to that location as well."

Looking at each other, the two dads give a slight nod. "Yeah, we can do that," says Sid. "And, Lester, I think Ben and I feel the same way about this. We want to be close by when the boys are found so we can get to them as quickly as possible."

Ben nods his head in agreement.

"Okay," the sheriff says as he turns his attention to the paramedics. "You fellas come with us and be ready if we need to take off fast."

The other teams begin heading out, while the sheriff and his small group make their way back to the shack.

Once Lufroy is tied securely to the same tree he had tied the boys to, Sid heads off to retrieve the sheriff's boat. As the sheriff sets his laptop on a makeshift table, Ben looks over at Lufroy. "You better hope both them boys are found before you get into that boat. If not, I'll see to it you're buried before you ever see another courthouse. That's a fact."

"I've had bigger men than you try and not succeed," Lufroy huffs. He's much cockier now than he'd been with the hillbillies. "I almost hope you do, though. My life won't be worth piddily-poo once I get back behind bars."

The sheriff, his back to the two men, can't bring himself to reprimand Ben for talking to the prisoner. He has a battle going on within himself and, so far, the side of him that agrees with Ben's statement is winning the fight.

CHAPTER 21

What's Their Condition?

Billy knows he can't make it much farther. The stress he's been putting on his twelve-year-old body is far beyond what most healthy adults can handle. The dizziness is constant now and at times his vision goes completely dark forcing him to stop in his tracks until he's able to see through the static that's been impairing his vision for the past half hour. His arms, legs, and back are burning like they're on fire.

And still he pushes himself. It takes all of his concentration to focus on the next tree in his sights. No longer does he look down to search for obstacles that might trip him. His brain can only focus on one single purpose—to reach the next tree he's picked out and to bring his friend home. Several times, within the last thirty minutes, he felt certain he was heading for the wrong tree and a few times, as his eyesight continued to play games with him, he saw two trees where there should have been only one. But he knows that he can't stop or fret over it. He must keep moving!

He's tripped several times since he injured his knee but has managed to rise slowly to his feet each time, refastening his friend against his chest to continue on his way. Without being aware of it, he's already kicked three snakes out of his way, and one of them was poisonous. He's just so focused—unable to even think of these dangers. The only thing on his mind is making it to the next tree.

Nick hasn't made any sounds in the last half hour, and Billy's given up on using the energy it takes to speak his name or offer encouraging words. He just keeps praying that his friend can hang on until they reach the next tree...and then the next.

To make things worse, Billy's long since felt that he's succumbing to the heat. He can't seem to remember exactly when the chills started, but he was aware from the beginning that this is the first stage of something that could very well kill him if he doesn't find a way to cool down and lower his core body temperature.

Still he continues on. If he stops, he knows his friend will die. If in fact, he isn't already dead. He doesn't even consider stopping to check, because he's so afraid that if he stops now, he won't be able to continue.

But he's forced to stop as another wave of darkness overtakes his vision. He turns his head to vomit out the meager contents of his stomach. Feeling his body tipping one way, he makes a move to regain his balance, which forces him to put more weight on one leg. And that's the moment when his muscles quit. He drops onto his rump, but somehow, miraculously, he's able to keep Nick's face out of the water.

Realizing that he's about to black-out, just like his friend, Billy manages to back up against the nearest cypress tree and wedge himself into one of the nooks that form naturally at the base of the trunk. As quickly as he can, he pulls his foot in, using his injured knee as a prop to support Nick's head. Resting his back against the tree, he looks down at his friend's dirty, sweaty, and motionless face.

With arms so weak he can barely move them, he scoops several handfuls of the bacteria-laden swamp water into his mouth. He knows he's used up his energy and there's no way he can attempt to stand again or he'll drown them both. It would be much better to just fall painlessly asleep.

"Well, buddy, I tried my best. I think we'll rest here together...forever."

Billy's overtaken by the fever from infection, and dehydrated from lack of water and sweating out his energy reserves. He's falling victim to heat exhaustion, which is rapidly becoming full-on heat stroke.

The last thing he sees before his eyes close is his wet and dirty index finger tenderly brushing vegetation from his friend's forehead.

Team-5, one of the teams that had continued the search around the boys' camp, is located about seven-tenths of a mile northwest of Swamp Camp. The men in this team— Spanky Gros and Creig Casteigne—have been friends since childhood. They're getting up there in years and, with the pot bellies they've developed over the last fifteen years, they're two men that are definitely suffering from the heat and humidity. But, the word 'quit' hasn't once crossed their minds. They have boys of their own and know that if it were their kids lost out here, the Landrys and Boudreauxs would be helping in the search, so they'll stay out here until they're ordered to call it off for another night.

Being out here takes Spanky back to the days of his own childhood when he and Creig were free to explore the swamp and create their own adventures. Letting his mind drift, he remembers the time when they'd spent a whole summer out here cutting their own trails. *Man, those were fun days.* Looking around him now, he focuses more intently on his surroundings. "Hey, Creig," he says, looking out at the trail ahead. "You see anything that looks familiar?"

"No," Creig says simply. Of the two, he's known more for his loyalty to his friends and less for his gift for gab.

Spanky gestures to a row of trees along the trail. "Look at these trees along here," he says. "The ones with branches only on one side. They're the same ones we cut to make trails for our 3-wheelers when we were kids."

"Yeah, sure looks like it," Creig says.

"Aw, man, I just realized, Billy and Nick are the same age we were when we cut this trail," Spanky says. Usually the one to find the humor in a situation, he can't find anything funny about this particular situation. In fact, he hasn't found much to laugh about since he heard the boys were missing. "God, I hope someone finds them soon so this can be just a fun story for them to tell, like the adventures we had out here."

"Yeah, me too."

They continue on in silence, each lost in his own thoughts, with Spanky in the lead following the direction shown on their GPS unit. Ten minutes later, Creig sees a flash of color near the water and stops suddenly in his tracks. He backs up half a step to get a better view between the trees and other vegetation. "Hold up a sec, Spank. I see something…There!" he says, pointing. "Something red—near the water level."

They veer off the trail set by their GPS and make their way toward that spot of color. As they get closer, it becomes obvious that it's made of cloth and tucked in amidst the shadowy trunk of a cypress tree.

Back at the bad guys' hideout, Lufroy sits in silence enjoying the turmoil the other men are going through. *They deserve it for catching me,* he thinks. *If I have to return to prison for the rest of my life, they should have to suffer too.*

Ben, sitting beside Sid, is focused on the two-way radio lying next to the laptop, mentally willing it to speak. Sid sits in silence, reliving special moments that he's shared with his son. Sheriff Leger, sitting nearby, is silent too, intently monitoring the movements on his laptop screen as if he'll be able to spot the boys himself, if he just concentrates hard enough.

It's now two in the afternoon—the hottest part of the day—and the sheriff is already dreading the possibility of having to call the men in for a second night. If it comes to a third day of searching, he knows the statistical chance of finding the boys alive. In fact, in just the past six hours, the odds of them being found alive have dropped drastically.

Once they'd captured Lufroy, the sheriff had contacted his office and instructed his deputy to inform the state police that the escaped convict was in custody, and to request their assistance in the search for the two missing boys. About an hour earlier, he'd spotted one of their sleek black helicopters flying slowly over the camp. Since then, he's only heard the sound of the chopper a few times as the search grid it's following brought it within earshot.

While he appreciates the effort the state police are putting into the search, he knows first hand that spotting someone in the swamp, through all these moss covered trees, is next to impossible. But, there's still a chance they might get lucky and catch sight of the boys in an area where the trees are more widely spaced.

Volunteers had been showing up at the Landry house throughout the day. The sheriff didn't have enough GPS tracking devices to give them, so they're on their own, searching without a preplanned route from the boys' camp. At last count, there were an additional seventy people searching in teams—separate from the ones he's been tracking

The sheriff is running the rapidly decreasing odds of survival through his head again, when his radio crackles and Spanky's excited voice comes through the receiver. "Sheriff! Spank...I mean, Team-5, here. We found the boys!"

As Ben and Sid bolt upright, the sheriff snatches up the radio. "Thank God! What's there condition?"

The delayed response instantly unnerves five of the six men around that particular radio.

"They aren't good, Sheriff," Spanky says somberly. "They're both unconscious and barely breathing. Oh, my...hold on a sec."

"Where are they, Lester?" asks a panicky Sid.

"Close to a mile from the boys' camp," the sheriff says, slapping his computer shut and practically throwing it into his boat. "They'll have to bring them out of there." He unties Lufroy and leads him onto the boat, handcuffing him to a seat on the stern. Using the onboard radio, he calls his office and requests a unit meet them at the marina to take custody of the prisoner.

As the last man boards the boat, Spanky's voice crackles through the portable radio. "Sheriff, Nick's been bitten by a snake. His ankle's a mess. Don't respond...just have the paramedics meet us at the boys' camp. We're gonna carry them back."

The sheriff immediately relays the message to the paramedics that are on stand-by at Sid's house and instructs them to meet the rescue team at the boys' camp. He then turns to the two medics in his boat. "I want you to follow me from the marina to the house. The boys will need all of you there to render aid and transport them to the hospital."

"Yes, sir, we'll be right behind you."

The sheriff starts the motor, shifts hard into reverse, and quickly backs the boat off the bank, spinning the wheel to head north, the quickest route back to the boat slip.

CHAPTER 22

Two Very Sick Boys

Sue and Annie sit quietly at the kitchen table staring down into their glasses of ice tea, watching the ice melt. Neither has said a word for hours. As the time ticked by after the their husbands left with the sheriff, they'd settled into a desperate and reflective frame of mind that's fifty percent prayer and fifty percent images of their boys.

They know deep down that the men are on the right trail, but still the fears they have are the same as those of their husbands—what shape will the boys be in when they're found.

They know nothing of Lufroy having been captured or of the new search going on closer to Lost Bayou. Their husbands had asked the sheriff to not share this information with them. If they knew that it was Lufroy's tracks they'd spotted along with the boys', it would just add more stress to an already extremely stressful situation.

A knock at the door causes both women to look up from their tea, their gazes locked on each other. Their world's have been in such turmoil the last few days and the fear that something is about to happen to make it worse is evident in their eyes.

Sue stands up slowly and makes her way to the front door. She opens it to the two paramedics who've been in the ambulance out front on standby for the last couple of days.

"Ma'am," says the man nearest the door. "The boys have been found and are being carried out by their rescuers. We need to get out there and meet them when they arrive at the boys' camp."

"Oh, thank God!" Sue doubles over with relief and bursts into tears.

Annie, hearing the news from where she'd remained in the kitchen, rushes to join her friend at the door. "Thank God!" she echoes with a smile lighting her face. "We need to get out there, now!"

Straightening to her full height, the ever-observant Sue, her tears subsiding, notices that the paramedic isn't smiling. "What's wrong?" she asks taking hold of Annie's arm for support

"Well, ma'am," he says. "Both of the boys are unconscious and one has suffered a snake bite. We won't know more until we can take a look at them."

"Oh, Jesus," says Annie worriedly. "What are we waiting on? Let's get out there!"

The paramedics lead the way to the waiting ambulance, each pulling a gurney from the vehicle and stacking it with the supplies they might need to quickly administer treatment to the boys once they reach the camp. There's no need for words as Annie and Sue, both looking determined, follow close behind as they make their way down the trail. They just know that they'll be touching their babies soon.

When the muddy trail leading to the camp makes it difficult to push the gurneys, the paramedics hurriedly carry the supplies to the camp, bringing them inside and stacking them in a corner. They rush back to where they left the gurneys, collapse the wheels, and carry them to the camp.

Fifteen minutes have passed since the medics have finished setting up their field hospital when they hear the splashing of water nearby. Annie and Sue, eager to see their boys, make a move to dart off in the direction of the sound, but the paramedics steady them with a hand.

"Please, ladies, let's wait here," says the same medic who gave them the news of the boys' rescue. "We need to administer first aid as quickly as possible and don't want to slow them down any."

Resigned to waiting, Annie and Sue stand there watching as Spanky and Creig struggle to carry the boys to safety, and then listen as the paramedic instructs the men to lay the boys on the gurneys. Gently setting the boys down, Spanky and Creig step back as the professionals, urgently shooing everyone off to the side, get to work.

Shocked by the boys' appearance, their moms watch as the clothes is cut away from their bodies, revealing the seriousness of their injuries. They can clearly see the ugly black wound and oozing blood from the snakebite on Nick's ankle, and the ghastly wound on Billy's knee, where a large flap of skin is hanging loose, exposing a filthy kneecap. Infection has set in and their small bodies are covered in red and swollen sores. It's obvious that they've suffered significantly. Annie and Sue are brokenhearted to see their babies in such condition.

"Are they gonna be okay?" Sue asks in a tearful voice, unable to remain silent any longer. "Why aren't they awake?"

"I'm administering anti-venom to the snakebite victim," the paramedic who seems to be the spokesman of the two says without so much as a pause in his task. "Both boys are extremely dehydrated and suffering from heat exhaustion, possibly heat stroke…Clint, we need to start the IVs," he instructs his partner, "then get them to the ambulance ASAP." Once the intravenous lines have been put in place, the paramedic turns to look at Creig and Spanky, standing behind the boys' moms. "Can you men give us a hand here? We need you to each grab an end of a gurney so we can carry these boys out of here. And, ladies," he says gesturing to Annie and Sue. "You two can carry these IV drip bags." He hands them each a clear bag filled with fluid, demonstrating as he speaks. "Just hold the bags up in the air, like this, as we carry the boys out on the gurneys. Are there any questions?"

Shaking their heads in answer, they all take their places. The wheeled legs of the gurneys are once again collapsed and the group begins to slowly transport the boys out of the swamp.

Midway along the trail, Annie, looking down at Billy while holding the drip bag up high above him, sees his eyes open just a bit. She squeezes his hand and is blessed with the hint of a smile as his eyes once again drift closed.

"I saw his eyes open and he smiled at me," she says emotionally.

Sue is very happy for her friend, but too worried about her own son to say anything. She focuses on his eyes but they remain shut. *Oh Nick, please wake up.*

As they wheel the gurneys around the house, they can first hear, and then see, the sheriff's car speeding down the highway followed by a second ambulance. They turn onto the driveway and before the sheriff's car comes to a full stop, two of the doors fly open and Sid and Ben come charging out.

They see their wives holding the drip bags above the gurneys and run toward them, needing to see that their boys are okay. Nick and Billy are out cold and a quick glance at their bare skin makes it obvious that they're not in good shape. The dads follow behind as the boys are carried to the waiting ambulances and watch silently as they're loaded in back.

Not wanting to get in the way of the paramedics treating the boys, Annie and Sue join their husbands and watch as the doors of the ambulances slam shut. Seeing the four of them there, looking worried and lost, the sheriff approaches and offers to drive them to the hospital. Grateful for the offer, they all pile into the squad car as the ambulances speed away.

CHAPTER 23

Two Days Later

The Landry family sits in somber silence. Sid staring at a small flying insect of some sort that has landed on the wall fifteen feet in front of him. Sue and Melissa huddle close together; seemingly as one, mother and daughter each raise a hand to wipe a tear from an eye.

The room is crammed with people. At least a hundred of their lifelong friends have gathered with them to offer their support. No one speaks. Each man, woman, and child feels the same distress as the Landry family.

The door to the waiting room opens suddenly and Dr. Naquin enters the waiting room. The Landrys jump to their feet and meet him half way across the room. The stress of the last couple of days has taken a toll on Nick's family. It's most noticeable on his parents. Dark circles under their eyes and droopy, slack skin on their cheeks now mar their once cheerful faces. And, poor little Melissa has been suffering as well. She's spent a lot of time in her room, crying softly much of the day as she thinks of her big brother and all that he's had to go through the last few days. He's a pain a lot of the time but still the best big brother ever. Sitting here now, just waiting and hoping, she's clutching a small, plastic helicopter painted red. It was one of Nick's favorite toys from when he was her age and she grabbed it this morning before coming to the hospital thinking it might make him feel better.

"Okay, folks," the doctor says, holding up his hand to halt the flurry of questions that experience has taught him are about to head his way. "Considering the amount of infection and the overall poor condition Nick was in when he got here a couple of days ago, the surgery was a success." His words bring sighs and exclamations of relief from everyone in the room. "However, the tissue damage from the snake bite was deep and we had to remove a lot of the dead tissue. He'll have a long road ahead of him to recover fully. But his foot was saved and, if he works hard at therapy, he'll be able to get back out there and play those sports he loves so much.

"I tell ya, folks, if Billy hadn't gotten him back like he did, Nick wouldn't be with us today." He pauses a moment, turning his attention to Ben and Sue standing off to the side. "And, speaking of Billy, he's one lucky fella, too. Luckily, the paramedics were right there to start the IV fluids and administer the first dose of anti-venom. Both boys were overrun with infection, which made things worse, but fortunately, bombarding their systems with penicillin worked perfectly. It's a miracle, I tell you. The excellent health they're in is the only reason I can think of that they pulled through."

The room erupts with the loud roar of applause. The Landry family is assaulted with hugs, kisses, and numerous pats on the back. The feeling of relief is overwhelming, not just for them, but for the entire community.

Ever since Nick and Billy had arrived at the hospital, the medical team had been working nonstop to get them stabilized. The news that the treatments have been successful and that Nick's foot can be saved are cause for celebration. Finally, they can all take a deep breath and get on with their lives.

Ben and Annie Boudreaux, huge smiles lighting their faces, walk over to the join the Landrys. "I think we should all go to Billy's room and share this news with him," a very happy and relieved Annie says.

"Oh, Annie, I think that's a great idea," Sue replies joyously. "Besides," she adds, with a chuckle, "if we take too long to bring him the news, he'll hobble out here on his crutches and whack each of us on the head."

The Landrys thank everyone for showing up to support them and explain why they must leave. They give a few more hugs to the friends and family around them and head off in the direction of Billy's room.

They enter the hospital room to find Billy lying in bed holding hands with the pretty brown-haired girl sitting in a chair pulled right up beside the bed. The young couple doesn't notice them at first, and it's clear, from the smiles and puppy-dog-eyes directed at one another, that at this moment the outside world doesn't exist for these two.

"Ahem," Ben clears his throat to bring the young couple back to reality.

"Hello, Hanna. It's nice of you to come in and keep Billy company," Annie says with a smile. "You two look so cute together."

Hanna looks down for an instant as a pink hue colors her cheeks. "It's no problem, Mrs. Annie," she says shyly. "Billy needs me right now and I can't think of any place I'd rather be."

"Mom, please," an embarrassed Billy pleads.

"Well, what your mom said is true," Sid adds. "And Hanna should be proud to have you as a friend. You saved my boy's life. You're a hero, son."

Blushing heavily from the compliment, Billy's eyes pass over the people standing around him and make contact for just an instant with each of those looking down at him. His focus returns to Nick's dad and a determined look settles on his face. "Mr. Sid, I'm not a hero. Nick would've done the same for me, and probably got me out a lot sooner. Now he might lose his foot because I wasn't smart enough to find my way out of there without him." A tear trickles down his cheek as a sob catches in his throat.

Sue, tears streaming down her face, rushes to Billy and gives him a great big hug. "Oh, Billy, don't feel that way. You saved my baby's life and the doctor says his surgery went great. He'll keep his foot and be running around with you in no time at all!"

The pent up emotions in Billy come bubbling up all at once and he can't hold back the sobs. Relief sweeps over him leaving him speechless. He holds onto Mrs. Sue with a grip that expresses so much more love and gratitude than words ever could.

A few hours later, Billy's standing beside his friend's bed, their parents standing close behind him. Nick's groggy but still able to communicate with those around him. This is the first time the boys have been permitted to see one another and they aren't about to let the opportunity pass without making the most of it. At the moment, they're listening to the end of Billy's animated tale about how Nick was able to estimate their location and come up with a direction they could travel to make it home. Billy seems most impressed by Nick's ability to reconstruct the map—using alligator weed—so he could understand the plan.

Everyone looks down at Nick in admiration as it dawns on them just how lucky these boys were that he was able to keep his cool in a life or death situation. Nick shrugs it off. *It's not such a big deal,* he thinks.

He's had enough of listening to the praises Billy's bestowing upon him and interrupts before he can recount any more of their adventure. "Enough already, Billy. Stop selling yourself short. Why don't you mention how you were able to navigate us to the exact location we needed to come out along the bayou, or how you were able to carry me all that way, even after you busted your knee? If it was you that got bit, I never would'a been able to get you out of there. I might have carried you a little while, but there's no way I could'a carried you in my arms like you did. You might not like being called a hero but that don't change the fact that you are. Not many people could do what you did.

"Anyway, I know for a fact that there's no way we could've done what we did alone. We were a team the whole time we were out there, and we won." This is the most he's spoken at one time since waking from the surgery and it's taken a toll on him. He looks around at these people who love him unconditionally. "I'm just glad we made it," he whispers softly.

"Boys," says Billy's father who, up till now, had remained silent. "It still amazes me that you two were able to work together to find a way out of every situation you found yourselves trapped in. That's the definition of teamwork, working together to overcome any type of obstacle. No matter if it's sports, work, war, *or being lost*. You two should be proud of yourselves. And, you boys helped to catch an escaped convict. If you hadn't pulled that plug on Lufroy's boat he'd probably be home free right now. But I'll tell ya, if you ever find yourselves in this kind of situation again, *don't you dare pull a plug*. Just turn around and head home so we can have the sheriff handle it."

The laughter that follows this attempt at a reprimand is interrupted by a knock on the hospital room door. They turn to see Sheriff Leger standing in the open doorway. "Excuse me for interrupting," he says with a smile, "but I bumped into someone in town that sure wants to say a few words to the boys." The sheriff steps into the room, followed by Mr. Pierre.

Dressed in dirty coveralls, Mr. Pierre looks like he wants nothing more than to be out in the swamp running his crawfish traps.

"Hello there, folks," he says hesitantly. "I just wanted to say a few words if I may."

"Of course you can, Mr. Pierre," Sue says instantly.

"Well…um, I just wanted to tell you boys that I thank you from the bottom of my heart for what you did. I was lost not knowing what I would do for the rest of my days. Those stories of the Rougarou kept me awake many'a night when I was a kid growing up out there with no neighbors around. And when I saw that man in the costume I felt all the fear I had of that monster when I was a kid rush back over me. I'm glad you boys proved to me that it's not real." He puts his hands in his pockets and shuffles his feet. He's not sure what else there is to say.

Billy is the first to respond. "You don't have to thank us, Mr. Pierre," he says, deeply touched by the old man's words. "We did what we had to do so you could return home."

"Yeah," Nick says. "We look out for our neighbors just like they look out for us, Mr. Pierre. That's what neighbors are for."

Mr. Pierre quickly wipes away a tear that escapes from the corner of his eye. "If you boys ever need anything, you just let me know. I'll be donating a whole mess of crawfish when you both get out of the hospital so you can be welcomed back like the heroes you are."

"That's mighty generous of you, Mr. Pierre," Ben says. "A crawfish boil is a great way to celebrate. We'll have to set a date and invite our friends and all of the volunteers who helped in the search. I guess that'll be just about the whole town." He chuckles. "You got enough crawfish for that many people?"

"You don't be worrying about that," Mr. Pierre says. "I'll bring whatever we need. Well…" He pauses and turns toward the door. "I guess I better get back home. Got some traps to run."

As the door closes behind Mr. Pierre, the sheriff steps closer to the group. "I relayed the statement Billy gave us to the FBI," he says. "They have a special task force that fights organized crime and they tell me that this Roscoe Clinton has been on their list for a long time. They've got a ton of evidence against him, but haven't been able to nab him. Roscoe's a wily one—he's got a knack for knowing just when it's time to change locations, staying one step ahead of the authorities. However," he says as he hikes up his gun belt, "yesterday they got a tip on his son Jeb. Seems someone at the hospital recognized Jeb when his wife went into labor and he brought her to the emergency room. Unfortunately, by the time the agents got there, Jeb had already left the hospital. They've got a man standing by for when he returns, at which time they'll bring him in. Hopefully, this will lead to Roscoe's capture and, ultimately, the return of all that stolen merchandise."

"Let's cross our fingers that this does happen," Sid says. "They put a lot of good people in a bind when they stole that stuff. Most of these folks can't afford to replace what was taken and they need it to earn a living."

"Well, I'll let you know as soon as I receive any updates. Now, go ahead and enjoy your visiting." He looks at Nick and Billy. "I'm glad you boys made it out of there okay. We were really worried."

A tired voice speaks from the bed. "Sheriff, thank you for what you did. If you hadn't organized those search parties like you did we wouldn't have been able to make it out on our own."

"That's my job, son, and why the people here voted me in as their sheriff. I wasn't going to stop until you boys were found. I'm just thankful it was in time." He smiles. "Now get healed up so we can boil us up some of those crawfish and have a real Cajun welcome home party."

Grinning at the thought of a big crawfish boil, Nick says, "Yes, sir, I will. Thanks again."

As the door closes behind the sheriff, Ben suddenly remembers something. "Oh, by the way, boys," he says. "A reporter approached me earlier about doing a story about you and your adventure. You're already all over the news being tagged as heroes. So, what do you think? You boys want to share your adventure with the world?"

With a knowing smile on his face Billy looks down at his best friend in the whole world. Nick smiles back then looks at Mr. Ben. "When I feel a little better," he says, sounding tired. "I think it'd be great for this adventure to get out. It's one heck of a story—part monster, part escaped convict, and part friendship."

Billy reaches down and places his hand on Nick's arm. "It's *all* about friendship, buddy."

EPILOGUE

Roscoe Clinton, head of the Hillbilly Mafia, quietly folds the newspaper and sets it down on the old scarred table in his shabby office at one of a dozen lumberyards he owns deep in the Ozark Mountains. Of course, his name doesn't appear on the paperwork at any of these businesses but the money still comes directly to him.

As predicted, he and his crew made it back with the stolen property which was quickly sold off. His son Jeb, sitting across from him, is now the proud pappy of a set of twin girls born the day before. Jeb's wife Marcy-May, who's doing fine after her ordeal, swore to him that she won't be having any more kids. Roscoe had smiled to himself when he'd heard that announcement. It'd reminded him of when his wife had said those very same words after their first child was born—she's had seven more since then.

"Well, son," he says. "It looks like that sidewinder Lufroy is on his way back to Angola. I knew he didn't have what it takes to get away. And, I'm happy to see those two boys made it home. They'll have one heck of a story to share."

"Yeah, Paw, that they will. How about that boy that had the messed up face? They catch him, too?"

"Well, son, it seems his name destined him to go out in a bad way. The paper says that he wasn't found but there were gator tracks leading up to where he was last seen. They say it looks like the gator drug something back out into the water, so they're assuming he was unconscious or had passed away because of his injuries." He shakes his head sympathetically. "I'm just sorry it was him and not that lying Lufroy that had to meet his maker in such a bad way. Poor Gator Bait, was just a mixed up fella unfortunate enough to've been born into a family that was too mean to teach him right."

Jeb thinks on this for a moment. "We sure are lucky, ain't we? I know it's been a long time since I thanked you for being such a great daddy, but...thank you. You've always done right for us and that story just helped me realize again how good a paw you really are."

"Why, thank you, son. That really means a lot to me. Now it's time you do the same for your family. Those two little girls are gonna need to be taught everything and you're gonna be one of the biggest teachers in their lives. All you have to do is teach them the way you were taught and they'll grow into some lovely ladies one day."

"I sure plan to teach 'em right. Well, I guess I better get back to the hospital now," Jeb says as he stands and walks to the office door. "You need me to help you with anything else?"

"No, son, there's just a few things I gotta take care of here, then I'll head on home. Go on, spend time with your family. I'll call if I need ya."

As his son walks out of the room, a smile forms on Roscoe's wide face. He sure is blessed to have such a great family.

But by the end of this day, Roscoe's outlook on life would be changed forever.

Lufroy Aucoin sits handcuffed in the back of a transport van watching through the driver's side window as they approach the archway with big black letters stretching across: *Louisiana State Penitentiary*. He squeezes his eyelids shut as the headache that's been building the entire trip reaches a painful level.

The headache had started when the guard sitting in the passenger seat started reading—out loud—the story the boys had given to a reporter. Every other inmate being transferred with Lufroy heard how the two youngsters had outsmarted and humiliated the bad guys. All but one of the inmates in the van had broken out in laughter several times and Lufroy can still hear the comments being directed his way from the prisoners behind him. This humiliation will cause him big problems once he's in the prison yard. He'll be painted as weak and stupid—and he'll have to fight many fights to change that in the minds of the other inmates.

Mexico is so far away that he's even having trouble holding onto the vision of his imaginary senorita serving girl. He hopes that she'll reappear someday soon because without her to remind him of what he thinks is the good life, he'll surely go insane. It's the only escape he has from the violent and unpredictable environment he's now forced to live in.

Back to the wheeling and dealing for cigarettes. Back to the slop they serve at meal times. Back to the constant necessity of watching your back. Back to the degrading strip searches…and back to the life of one who has no life. His anger rises with each recollection of what life in prison promises.

The van passes through the gates and Lufroy releases an audible sigh as he watches the men dressed in blue jeans and blue shirts laboring in the potato field. It's one hundred degrees out there, with one hundred percent humidity. Guards on horseback hold shotguns trained on these men to keep them from even thinking of making a run for it.

He looks down at his hands and a teardrop lands on his thumb—the first tear he's shed since the last time he passed through these same gates several years back.

He knows that his life will be spent in that potato field, toiling in the heat of summer and cold of winter—a never-ending torture to be relived every day for the rest of his life.

He spots the old wooden markers that stick out of the ground, marking each spot where a dead inmate is buried. He thinks the day they put a marker up over his body will be the only good day he's got left to look forward to.

As the gates slide shut behind him, he thinks of how close he'd come to making it to freedom.

If it weren't for them darn boys!

I hope you enjoyed The Adventures of Nick and Billy!

I thank you so very much for reading this book. I would be very grateful if you would leave a review at which ever store you purchased this book from. The success of an author, especially one as new as myself, is measured by the quality and quantity of reviews he or she receives. And perhaps just as important, is the fact that I take my customer's feedback seriously and use it to improve my quality of writing.

If you do leave a review please send me an email at MH@MichaelHoardAuthor.com, so I can thank you personally!

For all my fans who have asked the question of whether or not Nick and Billy will be seen again, I can tell you yes, they are currently on their next great adventure and you will be able to read about it later in 2017. Leave me a comment on my website if you would like to be placed on my mailing list to learn when it will be released.

Thanks again for your support. You will never know just how much I appreciate it!

About The Author

Michael Hoard is originally from Lafayette, LA. He briefly attended the University of Southwestern Louisiana (now the University of Louisiana at Lafayette), where he majored in art. When not working, he can be spotted on a lake or reservoir fishing for bass, crappie, and walleye. He lives in Middletown, NY, with his wife Kathy, to whom he has been happily married for eight years. He is step-father to two beautifully talented and loving daughters and grandfather to two beautiful twin girls. He believes nothing is as important as family.